Explore. Dream. Discover.

Explore. Dream. Discover.

By: Danny Bitter

Explore. Dream. Discover.

Written by Danny Bitter

Edited by Erin Oakes

Cover courtesy of Angie (pro_ebookcover) (Fiverr)

Published by Danny Bitter - dbitterwritings@gmail.com

ISBN-13: 978-1-7325324-1-0

ISBN-10: 1-7325324-1-9

Disclaimer: While all attempts have been made to verify the accuracy of the information provided in this publication, the author assumes no responsibility for any errors or omissions. Should the reader face any untoward website difficulties, it is recommended that they seek out professional technical support to rectify the same. The author will not be held responsible for any repercussions beyond the scope of this book.

Explore. Dream. Discover.

Legal Disclaimer from the Author

I acknowledge that this work is entirely my own. Any quotes by other people have been clearly noted and I, in no way, take responsibility for these quotes.

I acknowledge that the character of H. Jackson Brown Jr. has been fictionized and my written character, may not reflect the ideologies or beliefs of Mr. Brown himself.

I also acknowledge that *Life's Little Instruction Book* is not my work but H. Jackson Brown Jr's. The version for *Life's Little Instruction Book* mention of in this writing is *The Complete Life's Little Instruction Book* (Rutledge Hill Press) (ISBN 1-55853-490-3). I, in no way, take credit for these writings and/or quotes.

You can pick up a version of *Life's Little Instruction Book (By: H. Jackson Brown Jr)* on most distribution websites (i.e. Amazon, Walmart, Target etc...)

H. Jackson Brown Jr's "Explore. Dream. Discover" quote can be found in his book: *P.S. I Love You*

You can pick up a version of *P.S. I Love you* (By: H. *Jackson Brown Jr)* on most distribution websites (i.e. Amazon, Walmart, Target etc...)

Explore. Dream. Discover.

Explore. Dream. Discover.

To my mom and dad.

To her.

To those who delivered an infinite amount of courage.

To the part of me that said I couldn't.

Explore. Dream. Discover.

"In the confrontation between the stream and the rock, the stream always wins, not through strength but by perseverance."

- *H. Jackson Brown Jr.*

Explore. Dream. Discover.

Explore. Dream. Discover

Explore. Dream. Discover.

One

Before

I woke up early the morning of the trip. It felt like a normal morning. It felt like everything was running the way that the universe had planned it to run: smoothly. I looked at my clock: 2:37 A.M. What had woken me up? I didn't know. I laid there quietly, listening to the sound of my heart beat gently against my chest. The interesting thing about the skin, is that it covers up chaos, similar to the architecture of a house. Behind the skin of your body, you have roughly thirty-seven trillion individual cells working non-stop, so you can be you. Though organization might exist, there is still a lot of energy and power that most people don't realize. Most people take that for granted. The architecture of a house is similarly designed to hide chaos like the skin of your body. Just looking at a house will not tell you anything about the type of lives that exist within the walls. I want to believe God did this on purpose when designing the human body. We are allowed to hide our flaws and chaos within ourselves. For example, there is no shame in working tirelessly (like our bodies do), but there *is* shame in seeking attention for your fatigue. Are you working for the people around you, or are you working for yourself? That is why the skin exists, there is no reason to flaunt your hard work. You may be proud of it, but one shouldn't seek to brag about how hard they work. Each of us have trillions of cells that keep our body running and each of us have problems that we must deal with. There should be no competition of stress or any intention of apathy for someone equally stressed or hard working.

The world is a body, and all of us, as humans, are individual cells, working tirelessly to make our world continually exist. The world takes us for granted, and sometimes does not treat us the best, but we trudge on, understanding the greater good. Our galaxy is a body, and all of the worlds and enormously massed bodies in space are individual cells, working tirelessly to make our galaxy continually exist. The universe is a body, and all of the galaxies are individual cells, working tirelessly to make our universe continually exist. What is the universe then? Who does the universe work for? Is it us? Is the entire fundamental fabric of existence just a complex paradox that starts and ends with us? If so, where is the line drawn?

William Shakespeare is credited with the quote: "'Tis in ourselves that we are thus or thus. Our bodies are our gardens, to the which our wills are gardeners." I believe Shakespeare is telling the audience that what we are is up to us and how we use our bodies. How we use those trillions of cells is who we will become and eventually how people will see us. It's important to master their technique and use them correctly.

I realize that this is not the typical thoughts of a teenager on a rainy Friday during summer break. But I needed to plan. I needed to understand the significance of my actions before I performed said action. When I was younger my dad always said, "Think about what you say before you say it, Blake!" Why is this rule only used for speech? If we must think before we talk, why don't we think before we do? As I continued to lay there, my phone rang. It was her.

"Ann? What are you doing, it is 2:40 in the morning. Why are y-"

"I'm so sorry to be calling so early. Is there any way you can come pick me up?"

"Wha-"

"I need to get out of here. I can't keep this up."

"Ann, I can't go out into the night at 2:40 in the morning. What's wrong?"

"I understand. Nevermind, I'm sorry for calling so early."

"Ann!"

The line was dead, and I was angry. I didn't understand why I was angry really, she just had that impact on people. She was a complex girl, who wasn't fond of succumbing to the normality that some people had authority over other people. For example, her parents were unable to control her despite their continuous neglect.

With her mom always at work and never usually in the picture, Ann spent all of her time with her dad. Mr. Paige, however, spent all of his time searching for the bottom of a bottle. There were rumors around Middleton that Mr. Paige took his anger out on Mrs. Paige and Ann which was a difficult reality to accept. Ann wasn't mentally or emotionally disabled enough to have felt any lasting impact from that kind of upbringing. I just had to hope that the rumors were fictitious. Anytime I passed Ann's house, or if I was picking her up from school, the house always seemed inviting and unabusive.

I was never quite sure if Ann did the things she did for attention or just pure pleasure. While kids at school smoked harmful toxins that gave them a few moments of high, Ann was reckless. She seemed to get her high from the sheer adrenaline of sticky situations. This was both (a) inspiring because who doesn't want to live outside natural limitations, and (b) dangerous, because at some point that high is going to cause you to become addicted to living outside your limits. Those limits are the reasons that people can exist in another set of limits; those limits are called life.

I laid back down after the phone call and attempted to go back to sleep. I must have been somewhat successful because I was awakened at 7:00 by my phone's alarm clock. Frustrated by my lack of sleep and Ann's night time interruption, I mustered enough strength to roll out of bed. I looked like pure and unadulterated beauty. My hair allowed for a nesting space to nearby birds. My breath was a great defense mechanism to anyone within twenty feet of me. I was ready to take on the world...right after a shower. The shower is a wonderful place to think. There is nothing to do in there *but* think (I guess one should attempt to cleanse themselves). Whilst cleansing, my mind wandered to school (of all things). Starting my senior year began stressing me out a couple of days prior. During my other three years of high school, I was so concerned about keeping my friends and passing classes that I didn't get a chance to stop and enjoy high school. Growing up to the mature age of 18, everyone had told me that senior year was made for enjoyment. I hoped that was the case. *I need a little bit of a break from the chaos and frustration that is high school.* I thought.

I turned off the water and grabbed a towel to retain my dignity while I searched for a set of clean clothes. I grabbed my glasses and I proceeded from there, as I had done every morning that summer. Get dressed: Check. Pick up room: Check. Eat Breakfast: Check. Turn on the news: Check.

The news was, and is, the exact same thing every day, which, among other reasons, was the reason my mom never watched it. She hears the news about a week later than everybody else. This wasn't really that big of a deal because it always consisted of a traffic accident, a sports team's big upset, a celebrity flaunting their status, and the news of a death. That last one wasn't heard every day in a place like Middleton, however. We, as a town, have had enough hospitality to not run around killing one another. It was a strange occurrence when something like this was on the news. I watched longer than I wanted to and continued to feel perturbed by familiarity. I shook off the uneasy feeling and headed off to work.

Of all the places that I could have worked at, I chose to work behind a desk. I worked at the Middleton driver's license bureau. It obviously was not a prestigious job, but it gave me something to do on the weekends and after school. For the most part, I sat around in a tin building making copies of automobile information and filing the aforementioned information. It's not a horrible job, it's just boring.

I wouldn't call myself a boring person. I've always wanted to go on crazy adventures, but it was not plausible for someone about to enter their senior year of high school. I was forced to rely on my acumen to keep me out of trouble because there was too much to be done during senior year. There was too much to worry about. I had to make sure I didn't ruin everything I had worked for. I had to find a college to go to. I had to go to that college at a reasonable price that was affordable for myself and my mom. The scary part of that wasn't about the money, it's about leaving. Leaving will inevitably be the hardest thing that I will ever do. It's a scary thought to know that the last eighteen years of your life would soon be just a memory. To start anew is terrifying. When a neighborhood undergoes gentrification, everything is torn down and rebuilt. Essentially, that is what I am doing with my life, and I've never been so scared. Now, I know that "an ending is just a new beginning" or whatever, but that doesn't mean you aren't afraid when an ending finally comes. In the case of beginnings and endings, I prefer to follow the founder of Taoism, Lao Tzu's philosophy. He said, "New beginnings are often disguised as painful endings." I'm not a pessimistic person (nor am I a Taoist), but I'm also not an unrealistic person. I know what is attainable and what is not.

Note: This may actually fall under a few Taoist beliefs.

As I had suspected, the town was a little shaken up from the event that was on the news this morning. It sounded selfish, but I didn't want to know any details until after work. I knew that I wouldn't be able to focus on my job if I had heard what happened. So, when my boss came up to me asking me if I was okay, I acted like I couldn't hear her over my audiobook that I was listening to via my earbuds. She was easily convinced and didn't bother me the rest of the day. When I got off, I went to let her know that I was leaving. "Hey, I'm headed out, I'll see you next week?"

She got up from her desk and gave me a hug. "Let me know if you need anything." I smiled, nodded, and headed out the door.

I got off work around 2:00 and, like usual, drove myself home. The drive back home felt incredibly off. In fact, the air around Middleton felt thicker. There was a clear sense of tension in the streets and through the neighborhoods that I drove through. It felt as if I had entered the aftermath of a battle field that ended in a surrender with the two sides continuing to stare each other down. It was only as I got closer to my house did I notice that there was not as many people bustling about as there usually were. Due to the incident on the news, people's normal daily patterns were shattered.

The drive home from work usually took about ten minutes because of Garrett Morgan and his invention of stoplights. Had those stoplights never been invented the rate of my arrival would increase as well as the risk involved in me driving. That day, however, it would take much more than ten minutes to arrive back in the familiarity and comfort that was my home.

I was pulling onto my street when she ran out in front of my luxuriously garish Intrepid. I slammed on my brakes. The gaudy orange color of the car could not have been missed.

"Jesus, Ann! Watch where you're going! What are you doing?" She motioned for me to pull over onto the curb and I did.

"Blake, I need you to do me a favor…" She seemed quite desperate, but she was not panicked. I was concerned but was also relieved to know she was safe. The unpredictability of the situation was offsetting but I shrugged it off because she always had a history of being unpredictable.

"What is going on, Ann? What was with that phone call this morning?"

"I need to know that I can trust you." She replied with a flustered tone. "Can I?" She looked at me, anxiously awaiting my response.

"Ann, I don't kn-"

"Blake!" She interrupted. "Can. I. Trust. You? Yes, or no?" I didn't know how to respond. I wanted to tell her no! I wanted to tell her to relax, to enjoy the peacefulness which she so quickly destroyed. However, I knew it was no use and I didn't want to sound churlish, especially in front of her. So, I quickly and temporarily buried my combative attitude, took a deep breath, and carefully responded

"Of course, you can, Ann. I haven't stuck around this long if you couldn't trust me. What's going on?" I looked up at her and she smiled at me.

"You are in for a treat, Blake Harper."

After

I'm not exactly sure when I arrived home. As I collapsed onto my bed and let my sluggishness and hopelessness overtake me, I began to rethink the events that took place. *When I said yes to her, I didn't think this would be the result. If I did, I never would have said yes. I would have politely told her no and continued on with my life. Things would have made much more sense if I only did that. If only I said no.*

Before

I watched her slowly get into the passenger seat of my car. She was wearing a red tank-top and jeans; my favorite of her limited outfits. Ann never tried to show off her fashion acumen because it was not something she believed in. You could never have looked at her and noticed the lack of fashion however, because you were too busy admiring her charisma. She was beautiful, in both personality and physicality. Her character, however, was questionable if you didn't know her well enough. She was very outgoing, and it was something that rubbed off on the people around her. Whoever encountered her felt their confidence flourish as they held onto her company. There was an obvious dichotomy between her and I. Ann was the sort of girl who would not care whether you are excited to be arriving home from a long day at work. She would make you agree to a mysterious adventure that could take God-knows-how-long. She was the sort of girl who made you question the lack of excitement in your life. She was the sort of girl who had impeccable timing and precise diction. She always cared about the little things, which continually made her a bigger part of my life. She was the sort of girl who was an inspiration to the simple and boring mind I call, Blake Harper. She was the sort of girl who was sitting in my car staring at me because I had been staring at her.

"You can start driving again, buddy." She told me as if I were a small child who didn't understand much of the language that I would one day speak fluently through many educational conversations. I awoke from my trance and put the car into gear. As I pressed my foot down on the gas, she spoke again.

"So, what were you planning on doing this fine evening before I rescued you?"

"I was actually going to research some more colleges and maybe go visit my dad, thank you very much. I want to be productive."

"You *wanted* to be productive. Besides, your dad will still be there when you get back."

"I still want to be productive." I reminded her.

"Not until you find out what I have in store for you."

"Which is what, exactly?" I asked cautiously.

"Shhh, I don't want to spoil it for you." She taunted. At the time, I hoped she was flirting with me.

After

"Blake!" My mom rushed into my room yanking me from my usual nightmare. She hugged me, and I longed for the cathartic comfort that she could consistently provide. I needed someone to feel my pain. I needed someone to know how much I was hurting and who better than my mom? After so much confusion and not knowing what was real, I knew she was and she would always be. I finally understood that my mother was someone I should never take for granted. She will always be there for me, even when no one else is.

"Has the date been decided yet?" I asked tentatively.

"No honey, the family is still grieving, and everything is being figured out. I am sure it will be sometime this week, but you don't have to go if you don't want -"

"No!" I interrupted her. "I need to go, it's a final goodbye." My mom shook her head as she hugged me again. "I need to go." I repeated to myself.

Before

"Where to first, Your Highness?" I asked Ann, who was applying some makeup to herself via her phone's reflection. This was an odd sight considering Ann's apathy towards makeup.

"We need to pick up a friend," she replied, not amused at her royal title.

"Who? I thought it was just going to be us?" I was a little upset but definitely not jealous.

"Don't worry, Romeo, we need to pick up Ian."

Ian was my best friend since early middle school and we hung out basically every day. However, once Sophomore year ended, his dad received a big promotion and they had to move to Nashville. Ann hung out with us on a frequent basis. We would play video games or watch movies together. When Ian moved, she wasn't as upset as I was, but I could still see that she was saddened. She thought that the past was slowly fading into a distant memory. It turns out Ann was right because all that is left of those gatherings is the distant memory and recollection.

"Middleton to Nashville is about a 3-hour drive," I reminded Ann softly.

"You better start driving then," she chortled. I could have not driven. I could have told her I didn't want to play her game. I could have told her I wanted to go home and stay safe in my bed. As I opened my mouth to decline her non-existing offer, I looked into her piercing blue eyes.

"Please don't be using me," I told her gently.

"I wouldn't dream of it," she smiled. That smile was the only assurance I needed that nothing would go wrong. That I would not regret the next several hours of my puny existence, or that this wasn't just a fatuous act of chicanery. I needed a little fun, and she was my one-way ticket to adventure. The opportunity I had been waiting for had finally appeared and I was not going to let it escape.

It wasn't an easy task being Ann's friend. In fact, it grew to be exhausting many times. She always seemed to be running on energy enough for two people, whereas I never felt like I had enough energy for myself. For example, a few years ago Ann called Ian and I very late one night to go off on a spontaneous trip with her and her mom.

"My mom and I are just trying to get away for a little while. Would you and Ian want to come with us?" she pleaded with us. We were both fairly taken aback, not to mention tired from the day we had just had. We jointly decided that if she were to give us a little bit more notice next time, we would be willing to go. Much to Ann's dismay, she and her mom ended up cancelling the trip and she seemed disgruntled about it for the next few days. It wasn't our fault; we are just not energized the same way she is.

I pulled out onto North Main Street and passed the library and the post office. I remembered going to the library with my dad on the rare weekends that he was home. I always went straight for the kid's section and would pick out something like Clifford or a Scooby Doo action book. I know I don't seem like the type of kid who would read "Clifford the Big Red Dog," but there was something about having a giant red dog that seemed cool to me. Apparently, I liked cool dogs because Clifford was rideable and Scooby solved mysteries. It doesn't get more kick-ass than that. It also doesn't get much simpler than that. Little kids are so innocent, and they don't have to worry about anything. They just have fun and enjoy themselves. Why can't that always be the case with me? Why are the children learning from the adults? The adults should actually be learning from the children. They definitely seem to enjoy themselves much more.

As I continued to follow North Main Street and as it turned into State Highway 125, Ann situated herself in my passenger seat like she had always done. She took off her shoes, pulled her feet up in a yoga position on the seat, and reached for the radio. She had set all of my presets the first day I got my car, so she knew which radio stations were which. It was a familiar sight and seeing her in my passenger seat comforted me and made me excited for the trip ahead of us.

Ann turned to me as she continued to flip through different radio stations and said, "What's your deal, Blake?"

"My deal?" I asked, a little offended while taking back control of the radio station via the steering wheel controls.

"You are about to be a senior in high school. Don't you just want to let loose? Don't you want to try and have fun and be spontaneous?" she responded looking at me as if I insulted her by taking away her radio privileges.

"I could ask you the same question." I shot at her, still a little hurt by her comment.

"You could ask me the same question. If you did that though, we would both laugh at the ridiculousness of the statement that I, Ann Paige, am boring or unspontaneous." She clicked through a few more presets, even though I kept turning down the volume. We went on like this, back and forth until finally I accepted defeat and allowed her to take full control of her usual musical terrain. I felt like a fool for even suggesting the fact that Ann Paige is boring or unspontaneous. I thought to myself, *I am on my way to Nashville, Tennessee because Ann is so good at not being boring. Wait, I'm on my way to Nashville, Tennessee.* It finally struck me. Ever since Ian had left, I had contemplated visiting him but never had the courage. That was the thing, Ann was courageous enough for the both of us.

The first thirty minutes of the drive was not as exciting as I had always dreamed it would be. Yes, I had dreamed about going on a daring adventure and throwing caution to the wind. In all reality, however, the adventure I was hoping for was just a vast state highway. I'm not talking about a metaphorical state highway that symbolized the "stop and go traffic" that was my life. I'm not talking about metaphorical brake lights. I'm not talking about metaphorical flat tires that symbolize my failures. I am talking about a literal highway, with literal brake lights, and no flat tires.

I looked over at Ann and saw her laid back in the passenger seat reading a book that I had read an infinite amount of times: *Life's Little Instruction Book* by H. Jackson Brown Jr. This book was a wonderful guideline for my life. It is full of inspirational quotes and ideas on how to live an optimistic and fulfilling life. By reading this book and the many quotes inside, I have learned many small tactics to treat myself and others better. In fact, these quotes stemmed a vast interest of mine in other quotes by other famous or infamous people. One of Brown's quotes says, "Wear the most audacious underwear under the most solemn business attire." This is a fairly interesting quote. I think it means to look conformed, but underneath the conformity, hide your own bold being. I guess one of the reasons that I liked this quote so much was because it is who I am not. I look conformed on the outside and, on the inside, I look no different. Ann is a lot like me in that comparison. Her emotional and physical being are parallel. Unlike mine however, she is non-conformed on the outside *and* on the inside. Neither of us are listening to Brown's advice though. He suggests that we don't draw too much attention to ourselves but at the same time don't be afraid to live. I haven't quite decided whose way I like better, Ann's or Brown's.

Brown is also credited with the quote: "Remember that everyone you meet is afraid of something, loves something and has lost something." This is a quote that reminds me that everyone is human, including Ann and including Brown. I was curious, however, as to what it was that Ann had lost? More importantly, I was curious as to what Ann had loved? I, of course, hoped it was me. After all, "Life is slippery. We all need a loving hand to hold onto." (Another H. J. Brown quote.) I subconsciously opened the palm of my hand, hoping she would hold onto it.

"This book is a waste of my time." Ann declared, throwing the publication behind her seat instead of grabbing onto my offering hand. Instinctively, I reached back to grab the book so as not to damage it but was unable procure it through the air. This book was something I treasured, and I did not want my treasure to be tarnished. I decided it was best not to argue with her and leave my passion for H. Jackson Brown Jr. private. I reached for the radio and turned down the music. Ann didn't argue or defend her territory. (A victory.)

"You know what isn't a waste of time?"

"Food!" She finished my thought for me.

"What are you hungry for?" I asked.

"I'm good with whatever you want!" she replied. This greatly annoyed me. I asked the question for a reason: to get her input on what we were planning to eat. If I was going to get whatever I wanted, why would I have asked her? My mom and dad used to do the same thing. It would be like eight o'clock at night and my dad would get hungry and report to my mom the status of his hunger. My mom would ask him what he wanted to eat, and my dad wouldn't ever care. They'd babble back and forth until it's finally time for me to go to bed. I would announce that I was going to bed and they'd decide, it's too late to eat and they will just eat some other day. I assume it's a common event that occurs in most households. We ended up going through the drive thru at McDonalds. I ordered enough food for two, paid with *my* credit card and got back on the road. We ate on the road and I asked her if she wanted to drive. She surprisingly rejected.

By then we had been on the road for about an hour and twenty minutes.

"How much longer do we have?" I inquired. She pulled out her phone and began to type and quickly announced that we had about two hours left on our trip. I started to worry about my mom and how I had left with little notice. I worried about work and whether my boss would be mad. *What if this trip took longer than the weekend?* I worried about whether Ian's family would even be home. Amidst my anxiety, I made the mistake of expressing my feelings out loud.

Me: This was a mistake.

Her: Are you kidding?

Me: Yes?

Her: No, you aren't!

Me: How do you know?

Her: I just know! This is not a mistake, Blake.

That last part echoed in my thoughts. *This was not a mistake, Blake. This was not a mistake.* "Okay," I quietly said to her.

"Okay?" she asked again.

"Yes, I won't regret this, and this is not a mistake."

"Good." she sounded pleased. She continued, "Come on, Blake! You love this, admit it! You need this adventure. You *want* this adventure! This is what you have always dreamt about." I simply nodded. If I was being honest with myself, it was not just the adventure that I wanted.

After

I just laid in bed for most of the next day. I had already called in sick to work. My boss seemed to understand before I was able to come up with an excuse on why I was calling in. *Why didn't I just tell her the truth?* I was completely broken; physically, mentally, and emotionally. I wasn't able to sleep after the few hours I got the night before. Images of the previous day kept swimming in my mind every time I closed my eyes. I thought of the doctors standing there, telling my mom what had happened. I remembered waiting to go home. I remembered previous days as well, like the car ride to Nashville that felt like an eternity. How idiotic of me to compare those few hours in the car as an eternity. The true eternity was the few minutes that I spent awake the previous night in between nightmares. But I couldn't just stop living. I wouldn't allow my nightmares to become reality, I would continue to live and continue to be the new me. The me I was introduced to by her.

Two

Before

The biggest mistake that I made before I left was not peeing. I also didn't call my mom letting her know that I wouldn't be home for a while. *How long until I would be home? That is a good question that I'm sure Ann doesn't even have the answer to.* More importantly though, I didn't pee. Apparently, neither did Ann. So right after we ate McDonald's, we both felt the all too familiar sensation. It wouldn't have been that big of a deal, except for the fact that Ann told me we were in a time crunch.

"You never said anything about a time crunch!" I told her too loudly.

"Yeah, well now you know about it, we can't stop for another forty minutes."

"Forty minutes?" I asked incredulously.

"Yes, forty minutes...starting now!" The next forty minutes were horrible. I tried playing a game to pass the time which wasn't much fun.

"Do you want to play twenty questions?" Ann asked excitedly.

"What happened? I thought you needed to pee too?" I asked.

"I did! However, we can't focus on it for the next thirty-nine minutes and twenty seconds! We need to pass the time somehow!"

"Okay, sure we can play twenty questions!" I agreed reluctantly.

"Do you want me to think of something or you?" I asked her with my mind racing with random items.

"I'll think of something, and by the way, that's one question. You have nineteen left!" she laughed.

"What? No, I still have twenty! How is that even fair?" I caught the question before she did. "That wasn't one of the questions!"

"Fine, you still have twenty questions." She was still smiling. I had to think of something that Ann would think about.

Attempting to think like Ann Paige was no easy task. She was such a magnificent being, that attempting to be her for just thirty minutes in a silly game was an insult to her namesake. She read my mind and knew what I was trying to do.

"Oh Blake, you won't be able to think like me. My mind races too fast that I can't even catch up with it sometimes." She giggled as she said that last part. I don't ever remember Ann *giggling.*

"So, you are a tough minded individual. That's common." I told her, a little off my game from her giggle.

"Be tough minded, but tenderhearted." she retorted.

"That's a quote from H. Jackson Brown!"

"It is indeed, Mr. Harper." She was smiling again. She was breathtaking. She was so genuine, and that genuineness was directed at me. I felt my cheeks heat up and had to make a quick U-turn before they turned the color of her shirt.

"Was that a hint?" I inquired.

"Eighteen questions left, and yes, it was indeed." I knew what she was thinking about. I just had to play along, and I did.

"Is this thing in the car?"

"Seventeen left, and yes, it is."

"Is it full of cheesiness?"

"Sixteen, and yes, it is."

"Do you like this thing?"

"Fifteen, I do a little bit." I was on the right track.

"Is this thing full of insightful lessons for you to learn?"

"Fourteen left, and it does have a couple lessons I guess I could learn." I was done playing with her and proceeded to tell her what she was thinking of.

"It is 'Life's Little Instruction Book' by H. Jackson Brown!" It wasn't as much of a question as it was a fact I believed to be true.

"Nope!" she said.

"As a matter of fact, that just cost you five questions."

"Five questions? Since when?" I asked a little upset with her desire to win so much that she will make up rules. *I have to beat her now.*

"Yes, five questions. Ever since I made up our rules about eight minutes ago, and you are down to seven questions, sir, after those five I had taken away, and those two you asked after." I didn't want to admit it, but I was getting a little irritated. I was irritated with Ann, with her games, and with her made up rules. I had seven questions left to figure out what she was thinking about. I recited the knowledge that I had learned already in my head. *It is in the car, it is full of cheesiness, she likes this thing a little bit, and it had a couple of lessons she could learn.*

"Is it in the front seat or the backseat?"

"Come on, Blake! You can only ask yes or no questions!"

"Fine," I groaned (even though saying front would meant it was not in the back seat and vice versa). "Is it in the back seat?"

"Six more and no, it is not."

"So, it is in the front seat," I said thinking out loud this time.

"Maybe it's in the trunk." She was trying to throw me off my game.

"It's not in the trunk." I told her.

"Okay..." she said, as if she knew something I didn't.

I totally caved, "Is it in the trunk?"

"No, and now you only have five questions to go."

I started looking around the front seat. I thought some more. *What in the front seat is cheesy besides the other half of her uneaten cheeseburger? She sorts of likes it: she sort of likes cheeseburgers since she only ate half of one.* It sounded about right, except for the fact that no cheeseburger I had met had some lessons to be learned.

"Is this thing on my side?" I asked smartly, attempting to cut my search in half.

"It is indeed on your side, Mr. Four Questions Left." I believed I had figured it out, but I had to push my luck.

"Do you think this thing is smart?" I asked, putting a little too much emphasis on the word 'thing.'

"I do in fact think this thing is very smart. Three left."

"Did you force this *thing* to go on a crazy adventure with you?" She waited a minute to answer this question. Perhaps she was thinking on how best to answer it.

"I did not force it to go on a crazy adventure with me. It actually decided for itself to go on this adventure with me." I smiled at her, even though I thought in my head how untrue this statement was. At that moment, my teenager side took over and I lost control of the metaphorical wheel of my mind. (We were in no literal danger on the highway.)

"Do you think this thing is cute?" *What a superficial question to ask.* I wished nothing more at that moment than to grab the question out of the air as it headed for her direction. Unfortunately for me, our words are not tangible after they are spoken. I prepared for the crushing blow, but it did not come.

"I actually think this thing is very cute." She smiled at me. She didn't even tell me how many questions I had left because at that moment we both knew what the answer was. I didn't even have to say it. At that moment in time we were both connected and there was nothing more peaceful.

We played a couple more games of twenty questions to keep our minds off the insane amounts of urine that was being held up in our bladders. During my turn, I thought of my luxurious Intrepid and on her next turn she thought of the aglet on her left shoe. *If that didn't sum up our entire personalities, I don't know what else would.* I proceeded to point out to her that each shoe comes with two aglets. However, she pulled up her left shoe, and sure enough: only one aglet covered the top of one end of her shoe lace. Finally, after putting her left shoe back where it belonged, she announced that it was okay to use the bathroom.

"Yes! Finally!" I began to say. However, when I had reached about the second 'L' in the word 'finally,' Ann cut me off.

"We need to be really quick though! How are we on gas?" I looked down at the gas gauge, or whatever it is called. It was between half of a tank and a quarter of a tank because I had not gotten gas on my way to work, and in the excitement of the road trip, I hadn't really thought to get gas when we headed off to Nashville.

"How much longer do we have until we get to Nashville?" I asked, thinking about how many more miles the car could go without getting gas. If we had to make it quick, we wouldn't have time to get gas right now anyway.

"The GPS says we have a little over an hour left. We will be stopping in Jackson, Tennessee and there is a truck stop coming up on your left, right before you jump on I-40. We can stop there, but we don't have time to get gas." I nodded to show her that I understood. I had seen a sign for a truck stop about a half a mile back and figured I would stop there anyway.

"We should be able to get to Nashville on the gas that we have. You can say what you want about this dinky car, but the gas mileage is not the worst thing."

"That's good to hear," she said as she pointed to the truck stop.

If one has ever taken a road trip and stopped at a truck stop bathroom, they are able to recognize the horrors that awaited me while I made my pit stop. If one has not ever taken a road trip and stopped at a truck stop bathroom, then they should count their blessings.

Observation: Truck stop bathrooms are small, cramped, and exposed.

Analysis on observation: Is there a sort of petition that could be started to build bigger and better truck stop bathrooms?

Further analysis on observation: Where can I sign?

Conclusion: Truck stop bathrooms suck.

I raced to the car and started up the engine. Ann was in the front seat glaring at me.

"That took longer than expected."

"Sorry, I had to wait in a line, and then wait in line again to wash my hands. It was a big mess." I told her as I made my way onto I-40.

"Thank you for not becoming impatient and leaving without me," I added, turning up the radio as a little reward.

"I couldn't have done so even if I wanted to, Blake." she said looking out the window towards the immense highway.

After

When you are grieving, your mind forgets very normal things. For example, as I was attempting to make cereal to silence my angry stomach, I put the milk in the pantry not thinking twice. I only realized it when I was trying to put my cereal away in the refrigerator. It is interesting how human minds react to different events or situations in their lives. Yet, when you are put in a dangerous situation, adrenaline kicks in and you are able to perform crazy and superhuman actions. Grief affects you differently as well. Your mind is so focused on the grief and that sadness, that it has a hard time focusing on the normal things that we think about such as the preferred temperature of milk. Our mind is interesting. Brown tells us, "Be tough minded and tenderhearted." However, during grief, we can only be tenderhearted because our mind is not tough enough to handle the pain.

Before

We continued to drive on I-40 for a while. Once we had only twenty minutes left until we reached our destination, Ann pulled out a piece of paper and started to write.

"What are you doing?" I asked.

"I'm just adding to my list of things that I want to do before I kick the bucket!" She caught me off guard with this.

"You are only 18, why are you focusing on that sort of morbidity?" I was interested why the life driven Ann was so inclined to write a bucket list.

"I have told you about this list before, Blake. About a month ago, I called you up and asked if you would ever go skydiving with me, remember?"

I laughed. That phone conversation lasted a whole four seconds. I was laying in my bed studying for my last day of finals when the phone rang. I looked at my phone and saw it was Ann and answered it a little too quickly. The conversation pretty much played out like this:

Me: Hey, what's going on?

Her: Would you go skydiving with me?

Me: Right now?

Her: No, at some point in our fleeting existence.

Me: Uhm...I guess?

Her: Awesome, bye.

The phone beeped signaling the end of our short conversation. I reluctantly went back to studying. I was hoping that would be the phone call I had dreamt about, the phone call that whisked me away on a crazy adventure, not unlike this one. I assumed that is why I was so willing to take this road trip with her. She hit the nail on the head when she said, "You need this adventure, you *want* this adventure." *I have, in fact, wanted this ever since I met her.* Finally, after years of waiting I was given my chance and I was not going to pass it up.

"So, what sort of awe-inspiring, life threatening, and wild things are on that depressingly morbid list of yours?" I questioned.

"Well, what sort of things do you *think* are on this awe-inspiring, life threatening, and wildly depressing morbid list of mine?" I replied cautiously, as not to offend her.

"I believe that the actions written out on that list will never be possible due to their inevitably horrid consequences." *Welp! That was about as not cautious and offensive as one could be to a girl. I might as well have stopped the car and kicked her onto the highway, driving off and yelling about how ugly she was.*

Her face dropped as she said, "I'll have you know, I am very well educated on the dos and don'ts of living. Such as: if you don't want to be splattered, don't run out into the middle of the street. Also, don't go skydiving without a parachute!"

"So, I am assuming that neither of those things are on your list?" I taunted.

"They are *not* on this list."

"Is taking a 3-hour road trip to Nashville one of those things on your list?" She didn't answer me, and I assumed it was because she didn't hear me. Though I still began to wonder. Was she using me for this bucket list of hers? Why was she wanting to get things written off of the list now and not when she grows up to a more mature age? I began further investigation in my head.

If I was to write a bucket list full of immature yet exciting things to do, I wouldn't want to have those things ruined by maturity. I would want to do them while I was still willing to do them. People always talk about how things will get better when you become more mature, but I'm willing to admit to them that I believe them to be wrong. Albert Einstein once said, "I live in that solitude which is painful in youth, but delicious in the years of maturity."

Observation: Albert Einstein was not seen out in public often unless he was being recognized for something.

Analysis: Living in solitude is painful in youth because it limits the sort of things you can get away with because you are so youthful.

Further Analysis: Being "youthful" is a great excuse to make dumb decisions.

Conclusion: Maturity takes away your youth and along with that, your excuse to make dumb decisions, forcing you to make smart and "mature" decisions which inevitably leads to you becoming an adult.

I didn't blame Ann then, for wanting to take life by the horns, or however that saying goes. If I'm being honest, I'm probably *too* into quotes. I recite them way too often and try to live by all of them. The problem with that, is that many of them so obviously contradict themselves so I cannot succeed in that task. My homeroom teacher in school is equally obsessed with quotes, which continuously fuels my high for them. On that note, Joshua L. Liebman, a famous Rabbi and author once said, "Maturity is achieved when a person postpones immediate pleasures for long-term values." If I could physically shake Liebman's hand, I would. However, I sadly cannot do that considering he has been dead for almost 70 years. Liebman knew exactly what I had been thinking. Since my belief is that maturity and youthfulness are opposites and youthfulness ends where maturity begins, it is safe to define maturity as the focus on long-term values. That would then make the definition of youthfulness the focus on immediate pleasures. Also, having defined youthfulness, I have also defined Ann Paige. Ann Paige is a focuser of immediate pleasures.

When we were both Freshman, Ann and her then boyfriend Brett, snuck into school late one night and put post it notes everywhere. The next day, everyone walked into school and there was not one inch of that hallway that was not covered in post it notes. It was soon discovered that Brett was not actually involved in this plan, Ann just needed someone to take half of the blame. Ironically, the couple broke up soon after that. Now, I know that it doesn't seem like that big of a deal, but one has to understand that it *is* a big deal for new Freshman to commit something so inspiring. It shows all of the other Freshman that there is hope and that soon they will not be little, annoying Freshman anymore. So, while Ann and Brett received a week's worth of detention slips, the rest of the freshman received hope. Looking back on that incident now, it takes my breath away to see how quickly high school has flown by. With only one more year left, I kind of want to make the best of it. I laughed at myself, I didn't want to get all sentimental about the 3 most frustrating years of my life. This is similar to a prisoner being let out after 4 years of imprisonment and looking back at the prison and feeling a sense of belonging to the place. *Yeah right!* I thought to myself.

We were about ten minutes outside the city when Ann looked over at me with the most beautiful smile. "Are you excited? Is your heart racing?" she asked, very enthusiastically.

"I guess," I said. "It's not really doing anything actually. Except pumping blood, it is doing that." I added. She rolled her eyes.

"Why do you do the crazy things that you do?" I asked cautiously.

"What do you mean, 'crazy?'"

"I mean, the things no one else would dare to do. Why are you the one who volunteers to do it?" I was worried she would take offense to that. She didn't. When she spoke though, I was surprised on what she had said.

"Did you know, Albert Einstein once said, and I quote, 'I live in that solitude which is painful in youth, but delicious in the years of maturity.' What do you think he means by that, Blake?" I was a little confused, due to the coincidental quote that she happened to pull out. It struck me a few seconds later that we shared the same homeroom.

"Well," I began. "I think he means that maturity is the thing that forces you to make adult decisions. It is the time of youth where you are given permission to act freely and make silly mistakes." I had simply repeated what I had thought of about ten minutes before.

"I would agree with that. Do you mind if I add on to that though?" I didn't mind at all.

"Sure! Go for it."

"Well, I think the time of youth in our lives is also an opportunity to follow the advice of our Roman friend Quintus Horatius Flaccus when he wrote, *"Dum loquimur, fugerit invida. Aetas: carpe diem, quam minimum credula postero."* I was confused but I had remembered learning about Mr. Flaccus (if I could call him that).

"Isn't that the Roman poet Horace?" I interrupted.

"Blake, did you hear anything that I said after our friend Mr. Flaccus' name?"

"You caught me, I tuned out." I admitted.

"Right, so anyway! He said…" and she did, she repeated the entire Latin phrase. This was something I remembered translating, but it was filed away in the back of my brain and I did not have time to dig it up. I figured that Ann's pride would translate the phrase for me soon enough.

"Do you know what this Latin phrase means, Blake?"

"No, but I believe that you do, Ms. Paige."

"You would believe right, Mr. Harper! The phrase translates as: *While we're talking, envious time is fleeing: pluck the day, put no trust in the future.*" She stopped. I wasn't sure if I was supposed to applaud or if I was to just sit and wait. As always, she was in my head and she answered the question for me.

"You may applaud if you feel lead to do so. By the way, make this next left."

As I turned I said, "I would applaud, except for the fact that I am driving. I am safely clapping for you on the inside because I don't want to end your life after I have been given the opportunity to see your full potential."

"Which is what?" she inquired.

"Which is the ability to remember old Latin phrases and their translation from sophomore Latin." She punched my arm and laughed. I held onto the steering wheel a bit tighter.

"I am surprised you didn't stand up on your seat while you delivered that fabulous exposition," I added. Ann had always encouraged me about my unordinary interest in quotes. Being in the same homeroom class during that imperative year, she understood where my obsession stemmed from. She had even gone out of her way to learn a handful of quotes to share with me in hopes that I had not heard them before. It was probably one of the many reasons our friendship has worked so well and why I never cease looking up to her.

"Horace was a genius. Seize the day is great advice that everyone should listen to." She abandoned her yoga position.

"If that's what it actually is," I said.

"What do you mean?" She seemed confused.

"Well, we were told that Horace was a genius, so we just assume he is. We don't question the fact that he is a genius, we just nod our head in agreement and continue on our way. The same thing goes for Socrates, Aristotle, Pluto, the list goes on and on. There are a lot of so called 'geniuses' but why are they given that title? There isn't anyone around who can confirm that John Locke was in fact that brilliant and that philosophical." I wasn't trying to sound like I was passionate about this glitch in belief, it just came out passionately and surprisingly rehearsed. For the record, I didn't rehearse it, I was just trying to push Ann down a peg. You couldn't let her get too confident or she would ask you to applaud.

"If you doubt little facts like that, you might as well doubt history as we know it. History is like a huge pile of rocks, if you take just one of those rocks away, the entire thing can come tumbling down on top of us. Turn left up here. We, as people of the common era, are forced to accept what history has told us."

"I guess." I said.

It was quiet for a few moments, until I heard her say, "We are here!"

Three

After

When people experience a loss, the other people around them always say, "I'm sorry." They'll say, "I'm sorry for your loss," or "I feel your pain," or the worst thing, "Do you want to talk about it?" No. I don't want to talk about it. No. You don't feel my pain. And why on God's green earth are *you* sorry about it? Did you cause the death? Is it because of you that I am grieving? No? In that case, shut your damn mouth and let me grieve alone. God knows I've done everything else alone.

God. Ever since it happened I've felt closer to Him. I would allow *Him* to apologize to me. If He said, "I'm sorry for your loss," I would understand why He said that. I would believe Him, too. If He said, "I feel your pain," I would believe Him. I would even talk to

Him about it, if I was able to understand the reason behind the incident. However, it is not for my place to know, I just need to trust Him. I just need to trust that things will get better. I sure hope things will get better soon because I can't continue like this.

Before

I looked at Ian's house. *Now I felt it!* I definitely wasn't going to admit it to her, but my heart was racing! *The distance between here and home was actually realistic.* I actually felt away from home. I actually felt excited and *(do I dare say it)* adventurous. I looked over at Ann and she looked over at me. Every time I gazed at her eyes, everything around us fell apart. It was just us. But she always broke the world and put everything back together.

"Okay, Blake! You need to go up there and knock on his door. However, I can't go with you. I have some things I need to do." About a million light years away, the aliens floating around in space were questioning the sound that was coming from Earth's surface. After a little while, they would trace the sound straight to Nashville, Tennessee. Soon after that, the sound would be linked to the breaking of my heart. I was being used.

"Are you kidding me?" I exploded upon her.

"Blake! Listen to me, I will be back. I didn't use you for a ride up to Nashville, I swear. I told you in the car that I wasn't going to use you. You need to trust me, because I don't lie, especially not to you."

I was still pretty pissed, but I couldn't take anything back. *We were already in Nashville and I still haven't seen Ian yet. He'll be a little confused on how I got here, but I'll just tell him that I wanted to drive up and see how he was doing. I don't need to mention Ann to him at all.* I turned to look at Ann, but she was already walking down the street. *Good riddance,* I thought to myself.

I didn't want to show how hurt I was, so I attempted to disguise the pain with anger. It didn't work quite as well as I had hoped it would.

I started walking up to Ian's door when I began to think of the last time we saw each other. We were hanging out, studying for sophomore year finals, when he told me he needed to leave. The sad scene played out like this:

Him: Hey, buddy, I have some bad news. I've been meaning to talk to you all week, but I didn't know how I would be able to say it.

Me: Oh great, are you breaking up with me?

Him: Ha-ha-ha, really funny. No, I have to move.

Me:

Him:

Me:

Him:

Me:

Him: Well, say something at least!

Me: Something at least.

Him: Seriously dude, I can't do anything about it, my dad received a big promotion and we have to go to Nashville.

I was really proud of his dad, of course. However, I didn't like that his father's achievements stole my best friend from me. For example, one night we had made plans to play video games until our brains fell out of our heads (like normal teenage boys do, when girls still had cooties). We were just going to be regular kids, but he had to cancel on me at the last minute because his dad won some award and they had to go the banquet together, as a family. I told him that I understood and proceeded to play video games by myself until my brain fell out. Every time he had to leave to support his dad, I always felt a pang of jealousy. Why couldn't Ian's dad be absent from his family? It was a horrible thought, and I wouldn't want Ian to go that long without seeing his dad. Take it from firsthand experience, it sucks.

I grabbed the door knocker (his new house was fancy enough to have one) and knocked out *Shave and a Haircut*. I always did this when I came over to his old house. I waited for a short minute and knocked again.

From inside the house I heard, "No way! Only one guy does that to my house! It's gotta be Harper!" I smiled as he opened the door! "Bro! How's it going! Oh my gosh! Mom! How have you been dude? Come in, come in!" I crept my way into the foyer and saw his mom. She was wearing an apron that said, *The Last Time I Cooked: I Hardly Got Anyone Sick.* I laughed as I read it. She looked down at the apron and laughed as well. "Dad! Come in here, you'll never guess who just showed up!" Ian was beaming and wouldn't take his eyes off me. It's been about a year since we have seen each other, which beat the record.

Fun Fact: The previous record was three days, because he and his family went on a float trip. I was invited to go, but I got really sick and couldn't. We even went on each other's family vacations. If our family decided to indulge in the spurious fantasies of the theme park by going to Disney World, he would come along with us. Likewise, if his family went on a road trip to California, there would be room in the SUV for me.

I saw his dad turn the corner and he was also wearing an apron, though his said: *I Licked the Bowl.* I thought this was funnier and laughed again.

He began shaking my hand as he said, "Good to see you, buddy!"

"It's nice to see you too, Mr. Hall!" I told him, still smiling.

"Are you hungry? Dinner is just about ready!"

"Sure, if you would have me!" I didn't want to intrude on their family meal, but I did love the Hall's cooking.

"We would love to have you. I hope you don't mind pizza." Mrs. Hall told me as she pushed me toward the dining room.

"You can sit next to me!" Ian said pointing towards one of the chairs.

"Do you guys need any help?" I started.

"Come on, Blake, they can do it! I haven't seen you in forever! Tell me everything! It's hard to come by Middleton news here. How has everything been? God! I'm so excited to see you! I was telling Dad we should take a trip down to see you guys, but we haven't been able to find the time." Ian was talking fast and seemed a little too excited. I didn't blame him though, I was as psyched to see all of them as they were to see me, I just kept most of my emotions inside.

"Slow down, dude. I'll tell you guys everything that you have missed." And I did just that. I told them about my job at the license office and how boring it is. I told them about school and my timid attitude towards senior year. Mostly though, I told them how much I missed their homemade pizza. The Hall's pizza was a town favorite. Everybody who lived in Middleton knew how amazing their homemade pizzas were. I had even suggested that they try and start a pizza business, but they decided to move to Nashville instead. While I ate, I realized how jealous everyone back home would have been with me. I looked around at the Hall's smiling faces. They were listening to my every word and soaking up any and all news about Middleton. The smell of the pizza dough and melted cheese wafted in front of us, acting as a common ground. From the dining room, I could look out and see suburbia. This was much different than Middleton. Then it hit me again. *I was further from home than I had ever been by myself.* I chuckled to myself about how thankful I was for Ann's unprompted attitude as well as being vexed with it. I was thankful to be in the Hall's company once more. After I told them all about life back at Middleton, they asked about the car ride. I told them how easy it was and left out the parts about Ann. I wasn't sure why. Maybe it was because I was pissed or maybe it was because I wanted to be selfish and keep her for myself. I didn't have as many intimate moments with Ann as I would have liked, so the few that I do have need to remain special.

"How long are you going to be in town for, Blake?" Mrs. Hall inquired. That was a really good question. I hadn't even thought about what the plan was after I met back up with Ian. I didn't want to just drive home. The mastermind behind the plan had ditched me and

I didn't know what would come next. I was in no condition to come up with a plan and I also lacked the experience that Ann definitely had.

"I think I'll be in town for a couple of days." The answer just sort of came out of me.

"Well, do you have a place to stay?" *I need to come up with a place to sleep too? I hadn't thought about this at all.*

"You can stay here. At least for tonight," Ian said excitedly.

"Of course, you can," his parents agreed.

"Alright, I guess I'll stay here tonight," I said. I was still caught off guard by my lack of planning. It made me sick, and I got pissed off all over again.

I was mad that she used me. I was mad that she lied to me. I was mad that she lied to me about lying to me. I was mad that I believed her. I was mad at her, but I was more upset with myself for falling for her game. But it wasn't a total loss, she helped in some ways. (1) I made it to Nashville so that (2) I could meet up with my best friend in order for us to (3) embark on an awesome journey to discover myself or something of importance. I wasn't going to let it be ruined because she wanted to go play around in the city.

I felt a strong familiarity being at the Hall's house with Ian just a few steps away from me. Though the house was no longer the same, the bond between Ian and I seemed unshaken. We stayed up most of the night recounting silly memories from the late years of middle school to the early years of high school. I was comfortable and happy to be with him again. Though, as Ian talked about some of his new friends in Nashville, I realized that I should have taken this trip much sooner. I realized that I have already missed out on a large part of his life and began hoping that we would be able to reconnect again soon, maybe even in college.

I woke up early the next morning. The sun was already creeping in through the blinds and lit up the bottom half of my body. I grabbed my glasses and looked around the room. At first. I was surprised that I was not in my room. Instead of my posters of the New York skyline, I was met with an abstract painting that Ian drew when we he was in elementary school. I began to remember what had happened since the last time I woke up from a night of sleep. I could hear the stampede of the rest of the house through the guest room door. The Halls were already up and lively. This was a surprise, however, because my mom doesn't ever get up before ten o'clock anymore, and I don't blame her. Unless I have to go to work or school I'm not up before ten o'clock or sometimes even eleven o'clock. As the 14th Dalai Lama said, "Sleep is the best meditation." I 100% agree. I wasn't Buddhist, but I certainly enjoyed sleep.

It took me about ten minutes to finally escape the comfort of the memory foam mattress. Much sooner than that, however, I realized that I didn't pack clothes to change into. I called for Ian in the most formal way that I knew how.

Me: Aye! Dude!

Ian: Bro! What's up?!

Me: Do you have some clothes I can borrow.

Ian: You didn't bring clothes?

Me: No, I don't think that far ahead.

Ian: Yeah, I have some for you hold on. I can't believe that you were so "off the cuff" that you didn't even pack clothes! That's so awesome!

Just like that, I was able to count on him yet again. Also, it seemed like I sort of inspired him. I wanted to tell him that it wasn't my idea to come to Nashville in the first place. I wanted to tell him about her. I wanted to talk about how amazing she is, how beautiful, how passionate, and how rude she was to leave me alone.

"Hey, Ian! Do you mind if I hang out with you today? You could show me the town and the fun stuff to do around here." He looked giddy.

"Oh yeah, dude! Totally! We can leave after breakfast." I was sort of relieved. I'm glad Ian's social life is a lot like mine: non-existent.

"Cool!" I said. "What's for breakfast?"

Spoiler Alert: It was eggs and bacon.

For the record: I really like the Halls. I like them a lot. They are great and friendly people. They can even cook well, hence the world-famous pizza. However, they are not very good at cooking eggs. I know, I know, 'How do you ruin eggs?' Well it goes a little something like this:

Normal people cooking scrambled eggs will break 5 or 6 eggs and put in a little bit of milk to make them fluffy. They will then stir everything together. Then, they will put all of it in the pan and cook them.

The Halls, however, will break about 2 eggs, and put in a gallon of milk for each egg broken. They then pour it out on a plate and give you a straw and spoon for to eat your eggs with.

Observation: I was a little bit sarcastic when it comes to the Hall's eggs.

Analysis: I was sarcastic, but that doesn't mean the eggs are any less bad or any less runny.

Conclusion: The Hall's eggs are bad and almost non-edible.

After breakfast, Ian kept his promise and took me out to see Nashville. Now, I understand that Nashville isn't Los Angeles, New York, or even Miami. It's Nashville, but it's not *just* Nashville. During the "tour" of Nashville Ian gave me some pretty interesting Nashville fun facts. The tour kind of went like this:

Ian: So, over here is the exact replication of the Parthenon from Athens, Greece. It is the only replica in the world.

Ian: Did you know, that in Nashville it is illegal to own a pet cheetah?

Ian: Nashville was founded on Christmas Eve in the year 1779.

Me: *Just Smile and Nod.*

The first thing Ian showed me was the Parthenon. It was pretty impressive. Standing in the middle of Centennial Park, the replica of the Parthenon is the home to the 42-foot-tall, Athena Statue, which is also an exact replica to the one that was in Athens many years ago. It was almost as if the Greeks took the Parthenon and transported it to the middle of Tennessee. The main focus of the

Parthenon is to preserve an appreciation to the advancement and the beginnings of architecture. I know, it was a little boring, but it was definitely more exciting than sitting at home by myself.

After the Parthenon, Ian took me to see the Hermitage, which was President Andrew Jackson's Tennessee home. (Ian, is actually a really fun guy, as much as it doesn't seem like he is.) It was about one o'clock when we finished paying twenty dollars to tour the Hermitage. (It was really cool to go and see, but not for twenty dollars.) We both began to get hungry, so we headed back to Ian's house.

We decided to devour some delicious Reuben sandwiches and then proceeded to go to the park and toss around the Frisbee in the warm summer air. There was just enough of a breeze to keep us cool and make us look like skilled frisbee players. Ian and I both took off our shoes to feel the soft grass under our feet while we ran and played. The Parthenon watched over us and kept us in the shade for the better part of the afternoon. Other kids ran around the park chasing footballs and each other. The top of the nearby trees whistled and swayed in a steady rhythm. The world was at peace. As we played, we talked more about our lives apart from each other. As the sun began to fade over the field, the peace in the world began to fade with it. I knew that I could not stay. I told Ian that I would talk to him tomorrow. He seemed to understand that I had an urgent matter to attend to. However, as the great friend that he is, he didn't pry. As we left, my biggest hope was that Ann had found a place for me to sleep tonight.

After walking out of the Hall's house, assuring them that I had sleeping arrangements and promising Ian that we will stay in touch a lot more, I grabbed my phone and called Ann. By work of the Lord, she answered on the third ring. "Hello, Mr. Harper, how can I be of service? Have you enjoyed your stay at Nashville?" *Of course, she was being a smart-ass. She couldn't help it.* I thought.

"Please tell me you have sleeping arrangements for us?" As I asked her this I pulled the car out onto the street.

"Yes, I do." She then gave me the address of a nearby hotel. *She pisses me off, but I can't help but think about her day and night. What is wrong with me?*

After

Things were really different around Middleton. I was starting to understand why everything happened the way they did. I wasn't sure I would ever fully understand, however. I didn't know if anyone ever would, actually. It was certainly quieter. I looked around at the small town that I knew and was taken aback at how much smaller it had gotten since the incident. All I heard was silence.

Four

Before

I arrived at the hotel and found Ann sitting in the front lobby, obviously waiting for me. "Did you already get a room picked out?" I asked her as I approached where she was sitting with her feet propped up on a table reading a magazine. She was always able to make herself at home wherever she went. Maybe this was why she always wanted to be away from her actual home.

"Hello to you, too," she said, glancing up from the magazine she was reading. "I have not picked out a room yet. You are the one with the money," she said boldly before looking back down at her obviously intoxicating article.

"I don't have enough money to spend on a hotel room." I said frustrated.

"Don't you have an emergency credit card for a reason?"
This time she did not look up from her magazine.

"Yeah, I have one for *emergencies*, and this is not one." She
remained quiet and allowed me to be irritated by myself. Of course, I
couldn't get mad at her and soon found myself walking up to the
counter and paying for a hotel room. *I guess it was an emergency
that I did not have a place to sleep.* I thought.

I put my minimal supplies on the one bed as we made it to
the room. "I guess I should've asked for a room with two beds," I
told her as she walked into the bathroom. She didn't answer, and I
heard the water running in the sink. I walked towards the sink to see
that she was brushing her teeth and looking at me like I had just told
a really funny joke. Only after she spit out her toothpaste and swirled
a cup of water in her mouth did she give me an answer.

"I don't have a problem with sharing, honey." My mind
totally lost it. Morally, I was not worried. I didn't think anything
would happen if we shared a bed for one night.

"Oh," I said, trying to seem unfazed with the statement she
had just made.

"Is that okay with you?" Although there was nothing either
of us could do about it if I wasn't okay with it, she seemed sincere
when she asked the question.

I stammered a little too much as I said, "Uh, yeah. No
problem here."

"Before we can sleep we will definitely need some supplies."
She began to make her way out of the hotel room fully expecting me

to follow her. Which I did. We made our way to the nearest Wal-Mart, which was not a far drive considering those things are everywhere. I actually was curious enough that I decided to look up how many Wal-Mart's were in the United States on my phone.

Me: Hey Siri, how many Wal-Mart's are in the United States?

My Phone: Okay, I found this on the web for 'how many Wal-Mart's are in the United States.'

Me: Well that doesn't help me very much.

Me: Okay Google, how many Wal-Mart's are in the United States?

My Phone: According to Statista, the company operated about 6,363 international Wal-Mart stores in 2017.

Me: I didn't ask for international. I'll just look it up myself I guess.

I decided to try googling again, but instead I typed in my question and scrolled until I found a reasonable number.

Observation: According to the always reliable internet, there is close to four thousand Wal-Mart stores in the United States.

Analysis on Observation: Four thousand divided by the fifty states equals about eighty per state.

Further Analysis: There might be more Wal-Mart's in the state of Tennessee than people in my home town.

Conclusion: There are way too many Wal-Mart's in the United States.

I swallowed my pride and entered one of the four thousand buildings in the United States and was immediately blinded by the florescent lights flooding the superstore. Ann and I smiled as we made our way past the door greeter and over to the hygiene aisle.

"We should just need deodorant, pajamas, and a change of clothes or two," Ann said authoritatively as she zig-zagged her way over to the necessary aisles.

"We should have grabbed a cart."

She turned to me and shook her head. "Never grab a cart if you can carry everything you're getting."

I sighed. "How do I know that I can carry everything that I'm buying?"

"Because, you know exactly what you need. Plus, without a cart, you won't buy stuff you didn't need."

I just rolled my eyes. "Are you trying to be Brown? Because his instruction book is already better than yours."

"No, I'm not," she retorted." I'm just trying to show you how I do things and see if you're interested."

I laughed to myself and said, "I'm very interested."

My balancing act consisted of deodorant, pajama pants, a pack of white t-shirts, and for some reason a button up and new pants. According to Ann, you never know when you need to have nice clothes. We eventually made it to the checkout area and I only dropped my deodorant once. I made my way towards the cashier when Ann pulled me away.

"Let's just do the self-check-out."

"How come?"

"Why bother the cashier when we can do it ourselves?"

This time I laughed out loud. "Maybe because it's her job? It's not bothering if she's getting paid for it."

"Well, either way, it'll be faster to do it ourselves." So, as the whip cracked, I made my way to the self-check-out. I wasn't sure if it would have been quicker to have the cashier help us, but nevertheless, we made it out of Wal-Mart and back to our hotel room soon after.

When we walked in to the hotel room again, Ann grabbed pajamas out of a Wal-Mart bag and proceeded to enter the bathroom. While she started the shower, I laid some blankets down on the floor next to the bed and grabbed a few pillows. Soon, after laying down, I began to drift off to sleep. I sank beneath the waves of sleep before she had even turned off the water.

After

There is a lot of waiting around. Waiting is something I never was able to master. I was always told that I needed more patience. I am left now to wait in the incredibly loud silence.

Before

"Wake up! We have a lot of things to do today before we leave!" It was an unpleasant way to be woken up by an equally unpleasant person.

"Wow," I spit out groggily, "way to burst my eardrums. You are such a kind-hearted individual to wake me up like that."

"It worked didn't it, Harper?" I slowly got to my feet and as I did so, Ann handed me my Wal-Mart bag from the previous night's outing.

"Here's all of the stuff you bought last night. Hurry up and get ready. Meet me in the lobby when you think you are presentable enough to show yourself to the world." With that, she closed the door behind her.

I made it to the lobby soon after she requested my presence. I was looking, as she put it, presentable enough to show myself to the world. I had the deodorant, toothbrush, the comb, and Ian's clothes from the previous day. This was all I had prepared. Let me just say, there was an exciting beat in my chest that urged me to want more of this trip. She was sitting at one of the hotel's computers looking at a checklist. "What's that?" I asked as I approached the computer screen.

"It's the list of things I want to do before I die, and we, Mr. Harper, are going to get started on it. After all, H. Jackson Brown said, 'Twenty years from now you will be more disappointed by the things that you didn't do than by the ones you did do.'"

"Yeah, I know. 'So, throw off the bowlines. Sail away from the safe harbor. Catch the trade winds in your sails. Explore. Dream. Discover.' What is on this list exactly, Ann?" I asked again, hoping this time she would tell me. She had quoted Brown, so my curiosity only increased. In fact, she quoted one of my favorite quotes. This quote has so much information about how to live your life. It splits your life into three main objectives that could be easily understood. Explore. Dream. Discover.

In the eighteen years that I had lived, I had neither thrown off the bowlines, sailed from the safe harbor, nor caught the trade winds. My hypothetical boat had only taken me to and from school or work and as one might be able to tell from my random road trip to Nashville, I am tired of that uniformity.

"You are going to have to figure it out as we go along."

I sighed. "Okay, you got me, I've come this far haven't I? How many days should I take off work?"

"I'd say about four or five days, just to be safe! You also might want to call your mother and check your bank account." I ignored that last part and excused myself while I grabbed my phone to call my mom.

"Yes mom, of course I am…"

"Do you have clothes for the next few days?"

"Yes mom, of course I do…" *Nope*

"Do you have a plan for food and stuff?"

"Yes mom, of course I do…" *Not even close*

"How about money? Do you have enough money?"

"Yeah, I have all the money I've made working last week, and I have my emergency credit card." *Oh, man...that was a ballsy statement, but at least it was true*

"Okay, I love you sweetie, be safe. I'm sure you need some time away after everything that's happened." She hung up.

I turned back towards Ann. "You have until Thursday, and I need to know what we are doing."

"Oh, come on, Blake, you need more patience. Don't you trust me?" She looked at me with a smile that could only be described as untrustworthy.

"Not when you look at me like that. You tricked me into this whole trip, how can I start trusting you now?"

She continued to look back at me. "You can."

What am I doing? I thought to myself. Brown wrote, "Love is when the other person's happiness is more important than your own," and her happiness is the most important thing to me. It began to dawn on me that even though I wasn't sure whether I liked Ann, I knew for a fact that I loved her.

After

Immediately after I got home, there was a lot of local media attention. Seeing as we were closer than most people were, the news had been knocking on our door very frequently. They had been asking me about the last time we saw each other or if I knew what was going on the whole time? I couldn't answer that question honestly, which surrounded me with an aura of suspicion. They had to understand how difficult it would be for me to recall any memories with them, right? *Obviously, we were close. Obviously, I am distraught. Obviously, this is not a newsworthy story. Please, leave me alone and allow me to lament.*

Before

"So, this quote..." Ann was saying.

"What about it?" I inquired.

"Who originally said it?" I was confused about the question and wondered whether we were still talking about the bowlines. "Are you talking about the 'Explore. Dream. Discover.' quote? Because there's a debate about it."

"Of course, I am talking about that quote, that was the quote you were thinking about, right?"

"Yeah, but I don't kn-"

"The debate, what is the debate, Blake?" *I hate it when she interrupts me.*

I sighed, "The debate, Ann, is that there is a certain amount of people who believe that Mark Twain had said the quote and not H. Jackson Brown. This, however, is ridiculous." Ann just stared at me.

"Why is this ridiculous, Blake?" The confusion never went away with her. I thought to myself about why it was ridiculous. *I've held H. Jackson Brown up on a pedestal for such a long time, that I assumed that he said this amazing quote. I was not a big fan of Mark Twain and I didn't want to give him the credit.* I stuttered. The truth was, I didn't know why I thought this was ridiculous. That lack of reasoning, coupled with the lack of evidence defeated my opportunity to hold an opinion on the matter.

Ann broke the silence. "This sounds like something that we need to look into. We need to solve this worldwide issue, and I know just where to start!"

Ever since I learned the quandary of my favorite quote, I grew obsessed with its origins and always wanted to set the record straight. So, when Ann suggested we do just that, I didn't hesitate. This was my dream adventure with my dream companion.

It's common knowledge that Samuel Longhorne Clemens went by the pseudonym of Mark Twain as an author. It is also common knowledge that Samuel Clemens grew up in Hannibal, Missouri. So, where were we heading? The Catoosa Wildlife Management Area in Tennessee. So, after checking out of the hotel, we get back into the Intrepid and begin our 2-hour car ride towards Catoosa by jumping on I-40. Just like that, we are back in the car together and I'm listening to her philosophical beliefs about life and death once more.

"...he literally said, "Explore. Dream. Discover." and that's exactly what we're doing! In twenty years, are you going to be disappointed by this, Blake?" Before I could even open my mouth, she was talking again. "Of course not. That is ridiculous." She rolled down her window and smiled outside while her hair blew violently in the wind.

I pulled her back in as I spoke, "You said 'he.'"

"What?"

I repeated myself. "You said 'he.' What 'he' are you talking about? Twain or Jackson?"

Observation: Twain is well known for his satirical writing style.

Analysis on observation: The Explore. Dream. Discover quote, is not satirical.

Conclusion #1: Problem solved, Twain didn't write one of my all-time favorite quotes.

Confession: I have only read *Tom Sawyer* and the *Celebrated Jumping Frog of Calaveras County.*

Analysis on Confession: Since I haven't read much of Twain, I probably shouldn't judge him so harshly.

Conclusion #2: I shouldn't judge so much.

We continued driving through the lovely volunteer state. While we did this, I realized something that had slowly crept up on me since I picked up Ann for the "adventure." I'd concluded that everyone wants an adventure, but not everyone wants to want an adventure. It's like this: for years (eighteen to be exact) I'd focused on my upcoming future. I had thought that I'd wanted to go on this life altering, self-discovering, "throw caution to the wind-esque" journey. And that was true, I did want that. But so does everyone. The difference between people like me and people like Ann, is that she always wanted to *want* that adventure. She embraced it and seized all opportunities for the thrill. People like me, on the other hand, are scared of what an adventure might mean. The Blakes of this world try to bury their desire for freedom and thrill (a few great attributes of any adventure). The Anns of this world embrace it. So, I guess we should all embrace the feeling? Maybe we'll all live more exciting lives? *Do I start to change my person into the person Ann wants me to be? I don't know.* I look at her, while I was having my minor and extremely early midlife crisis. She was just sitting there looking out the slightly cracked window. Her hair was blowing very beautifully just enough to where I could see her face. It was soft and gorgeous. Again, not because she artificially made it that way, but because she believed she was beautiful to herself. She didn't care whether guys like me or guys not like me thought she was beautiful, the only person she had to convince was herself, and as she convinced herself, she convinced everyone else.

After a while of driving, I say, "Do you know how far we are from the Catoosa Wildlife?" She looked over at me while I asked the question.

"I'm not sure, I will look out for a sign.

"Can you just look it up on your phone? I'll be able to plan accordingly with an approximate time." I told her this while I began to feel my bladder creeping up on me and the horrible visions of truck stop bathrooms flashed through my mind. I shivered.

"I am not going to look it up on my phone," she said as she literally crossed her arms. *Why was she such a child?*

"Fine," I told her, "I will look it up on my phone." I reached into my pocket for my phone when she screamed.

"Blake Harper! Don't you dare think about pulling your phone out while you are driving! You could hurt someone else or yourself!" I just looked at her, she got heated very quickly. "I'm serious, Blake! Just wait for a road sign." She kept her arms crossed and looked back out the cracked window. Her face was very red. I continued to look at the road. My phone remained in my pocket.

As everyone at one point in their life will discover, in the fight between your bladder and you, there is no chance at victory. So, yes, we stopped again for a bathroom and some gas. This time, however, we stopped at a nicer looking gas station, and I was confident about the cleanliness of the bathrooms as I made my way toward the back of the store. Much to my dismay, the men's restroom was "under maintenance." I audibly groaned as I made my way back to the car. I grabbed Ann and instructed her to stand guard. I walked past the cashier at the counter and she looked at me curiously as I finished my instructions to Ann. I guess she knew what I was up to, and felt violated, I know I sure did.

"...all I need for you to do is stand in front of the door while I use the restroom. I don't need any random women walking in on me."

"Well," Ann began, "it wouldn't be a surprise to you considering you are using the women's bathroom."

"I don't have a choice," I explained. But with that, I entered the women's restroom. There was only one toilet and one sink, and it was not much nicer than any men's room I've been to. As I was washing my hands the door opened and the cashier walked in. When she saw me, she stumbled back, gasped, and then quickly left. I followed her with my valid excuses, but she ignored me. I quickly left and headed back to the car flushed with embarrassment and anger.

I made it back to the car and Ann was sitting in the front seat. "Where did you go?" I yelled at her as I started the car.

"There were not any women around, so I figured you would be fine."

"Yeah, well, the cashier walked in on me!" I said, reliving the nightmarish feeling in my mind. Ann laughed. I shook my head angrily and headed back for the highway.

As Ann and I both calmed down, she turned to me and said, "Why didn't you lock the door?" I sighed, and we continued to drive in silence.

Five

Before

We reached Catoosa at around noon. We drove around for a little bit until we found a campsite and Ann told me that was where we needed to go. I drove up to the entrance, paid fifty dollars for the campsite and tent rental, and handed Ann our campsite ticket. I drove down and began looking for site number 48 as Ann attached our ticket to the rearview mirror. Eventually, I found our campsite and backed in the Intrepid. After I turned off the ignition, I looked over at her and she was grinning ear from ear. She then pulled out her list and crossed something off. As she put it in the glove compartment, she looked back at me and asked, "Are you excited? How often are you able to go camping?" I told her that it wasn't often my family went camping. Mostly because of my dad's absence and the fact that my mom doesn't know how to set everything up, or trust me to do it for her. Her smile faded. "Well, that was a gloomier answer than I was hoping for. Regardless, now we get to go camping! Everything we need is pretty much already in the tent. We may need to go grocery shopping, but other than that, we don't need to buy much." Before we went into the tent we headed back out onto the main road to look for a Wal-Mart. Sadly, one of the four thousand Wal-Marts was not located near Catoosa but there was a nice convenience shop that had pretty much everything we needed. We ended up buying a flashlight and some batteries, some fruit, a couple cans of beans, two packages of hotdogs, two packages of buns, a pack of water, and some marshmallows. We put down the groceries on the counter in front of an elderly woman. She was just tall enough to see over the counter. Her hair seemed to be curled by traditional overnight curlers and she wore a polka-dotted apron while she scanned our much-needed supplies. After she was done, she told us the total with a genuine smile. I paid with my credit card and cried for the upcoming bill at the end of the month. I understood that it wasn't good to spend your money like this, but it was worth it if it was for her. It's like what H. Jackson Brown Jr. said, "Remember that the happiest people in the world are not those getting more but giving more." At the time, I was giving way more than I was getting.

The convenience store was a little further than we had liked, but we finally made it back to the tent and it was nearing two o'clock. We unloaded the stuff from the Intrepid and headed for the tent. When we entered the tent we immediately saw the problem and I may or may not have audibly groaned. Unfortunately for me, there was only one sleeping bag in the tent. Fortunately for Ann it was a large sleeping bag, so I was sure she would be nice and cozy. "Well, it looks like we are just going to have to share, Blake," she said as she put down the grocery bag she was carrying.

"You've got to be kidding me." I said as I put down the pack of water.

"It's not that big of a deal! You'll be fine, don't worry, I don't bite," she laughed.

Too bad, I thought to myself.

After

People say they experience grief more often than they actually do. They experience grief at the loss of a job, a harsh breakup, or a bad test. They need to grow up. The Webster Dictionary definition of grief is: deep sorrow, especially caused by someone's death. I'm sorry about your job, you'll find another one. I'm sorry about your breakup, you'll find someone else. I'm sorry about your test, maybe next time. What the hell are people supposed to say to me? I'm sorry about your loss, maybe next time? I'll find someone else? It's not about finding; it's about being found.

The milieu of Middleton was completely transformed into a somber atmosphere. Before, there were people walking busily along the streets and carrying groceries and sure about the future and the upcoming events that were to take place. But after, it wasn't the same. People still needed to eat so they were still walking around busily with groceries, but there was an uncertain feeling that filled the air. No one was sure of what is to come. With the incident happening so sudden, no one could be certain of anything anymore. A void was left in the middle of the streets that was usually home to gossip and normality. No one was sure when things would get back to normal or if they ever would.

Before

Note: Nothing happened in the tent.

Note: Nothing was going to happen in the tent.

Note: I didn't sleep in the sleeping bag, I slept on the floor.

Note: I didn't get any sleep and I was extremely tired.

Note: Writing a "Note List" and using "Note" four times (now five) destroys Shakespeare's rule of three. Noted. I will now cease the "Note list."

We are both awake by eight the next morning and only one of us actually awoke. She seemed fairly chipper. I was eating some of the fruit that we bought at the convenience store as she began to go through the game plan of the day with me. "So, we are going to find Brown today and ask him about the quote."

"And, just how are we going to find him?" I asked, taking a bite out of my apple that was a little bit too juicy and sprayed my chin with apple juice. I wiped it off with my sleeve as she spoke.

"He has a cabin that shouldn't be too far from the campsite. I think that if we ask around people will have heard of him." I agreed to go along with her plan (like always) and we packed the Intrepid back up and headed into town again, this time trying to find "touristy" stops.

Everywhere that we went, Ann refused to be the one who asked about H. Jackson Brown. So, I had to be the one to do it. The first couple of times, I was embarrassed when they looked at me like I was crazy. The few people that did hear of him, reminded me that he was a recluse, and no one has heard from him in years. The others that hadn't heard of him were for the most part really polite. They would say things like, "No, I'm sorry sir, I have not heard of him. Does he live around here?" Those were preferred responses.

I was starting to get really discouraged as the day crept closer to sundown. We had pretty much driven in a huge circle and the car needed gas. We found ourselves back at the convenience store that doubled as a gas station that we had stopped at the day before to get supplies. (i.e. apples, marshmallows…you know, the usual).

Of course, Ann made me pump, and when I asked her to go in and ask if they've heard of H. Jackson Brown, she made me do that, too. So, after pumping my gas, I headed back into the convenience shop. The lady working at the counter was the same sweet older lady that told me my shocking total the day before. She recognized me.

"Well, look who it is, back in my shop again. Do you need more marshmallows?" I told her that I was okay, and I tried to ask about Brown. But instead I began introducing myself to her. I'm not sure why I started doing it, but she seemed so approachable and kind, and I felt like this is what I needed to do. She responded in a similar manner. "Nice to meet you, Blake. My name is Rosemary. Where are you from?"

"Uhm, Middleton." I said, a little more shyly at this point. I'm not the best conversationalist.

"Middleton," she repeated. The word held in the air between us. Middleton: my home and the place of my memories; all held in a single, ten-letter word, that floated there over the counter between

Rosemary and me. "You are quite a ways from home, aren't you, darling? What are you doing here?" She looked at me kindly. She wasn't judging. She wasn't assuming, she didn't have any ultimatum for asking. She was just sweetly curious. I felt like I could trust her. She hadn't given me any reason not to trust her, so I started to talk. I talked about everything that had happened so far. I told her about Ann interrupting my drive home, ditching me once we got to Ian's house, only getting one hotel room, and not preparing groceries for the camping trip. I told her every doubt that I had been having since I let her get into the car after work. Rosemary was kind enough to listen to what I had to say and only interrupted me twice to check people out. After I had finished, she gave me a bottle of water and refused to let me pay for it. I thanked her and started to head out saying that I had to begin to prepare for our journey back. As I headed out she said, "The best preparation for tomorrow is doing your best today. Things will begin to look up for you." I turned around immediately having recognized the quote she had recited although I couldn't place who had said it. I gave her a suspicious look and she responded with a smile.

I headed back to the car and entered the passenger seat. Ann was sitting there lost in the H. Jackson Brown book again. I told her that I had found nothing, but she wasn't listening to me.

"Alright, I guess I'll head back to the campground, so we can grab our stuff." I was about to start the car when Ann spoke up.

"The best preparation for tomorrow is doing your best today. Have you heard that quote before? I didn't know if Brown said that quote, but I remember it being on our wall in homeroom." I sat there speechless for a second.

"Rosemary just recited that quote while I was in the convenience store."

"Who's Rosemary?" Ann questioned me as if she knew something I did not.

"She was the nice woman at the checkout counter. Why do you ask?" I was growing ever more curious. Ann simply handed the book to me and told me to start reading. I took the book and flipped past the copyright laws and the dedication and began reading.

"1. compliment three people every day. 2. have a dog. 3..."

She interrupted me, as usual. "You've already missed it, Blake. Try again." I stopped and looked at her for a moment. Why couldn't she just tell me what I missed? Why does she have to talk in riddles with me? I looked at the cover again, examining it to see what I had missed. I looked back at her as I felt her eyes on me performing this task. She was shaking her head, so I flipped open the book. I perused the copyright information and eventually moved on to the dedication page. It was dedicated to his son who was college bound, but this didn't strike me as unusual or enlightening by any means.

"What does this have to do with the woman behind the counter?" I looked at Ann for an answer. She pulled out her phone and looked up H. Jackson Brown Jr.

After

I stood next to my mom at the burial and she grabbed my hand after the blessing had been given. As the coffins made their way into the ground I choked up, but respectfully held it in. After it was over, and we were dismissed, I began to pull my suit jacket back on.

Six

Before

Under the biographical section of H. Jackson Brown Jr, it listed his personal information. Next to his spouse the name Rosemary C. Brown was written. My jaw dropped to the floor in astonishment. I knew I had recognized the name, but I couldn't put coherent thoughts together. I needed to go back into the store and talk to her again. As I made my way out of the car and headed back into the convenience store, I remembered my homeroom teacher mentioning that Brown had a wife and I couldn't believe I had forgotten about it. I was just about ten yards from the door when I saw her heading to her car to leave for the night. "Rosemary!" I shouted and picked up my pace. She didn't hear me because she began rummaging for her keys in her purse. I ran up to her just before she got into her vehicle. "What do you call bears with no ears?" I asked her too forcefully.

"I beg your pardon?" She seemed a little confused and I didn't blame her.

"B." I said, without pausing for laughter. "What's the resemblance between a red apple and a green apple?" She waited for my answer this time and I gave it to her quickly. "They are both red, except the green one." This time I did slightly pause for the laugh. "A dyslexic man walks into a bra." I finished and there was a moment of silence.

"You learned three clean jokes, didn't you?" she asked me kindly. I responded with a recitation of Life's Little Instruction book.

"Number 21, learn three clean jokes." I continued, "Lucky for me he didn't say they had to be any good." She laughed again.

Rosemary and I planned on meeting up for ice cream at the Catoosa Creamery the following day. I thanked her, shook her hand, and watched her drive away. The car was traveling toward a man that I looked up to intensely, and I couldn't look away.

"Well, well, well," Ann started as she walked up towards me, "that is the biggest smile I think I've ever seen on your face." I blushed and finally did looked away. I couldn't believe our luck. I was absolutely speechless. "Okay, Smiles, let's go find a place to sleep for the night. That is, if you can even fall asleep. You might be too excited." I yawned and looked at her again,

"I didn't sleep much last night, so I think I'll be able to manage a few hours of rest. Just promise me we aren't sleeping in a tent again." She laughed and gave us permission to find a hotel for the evening. We picked a small hotel that was fairly close to the Catoosa Creamery and began to settle in for the evening after our long day of trying to find Brown. Ann took a shower and I grabbed a paper and pen and began to write questions that I had for Brown. The first question was incredibly obvious, and it posed the question of the quote. I was finally going to be able to prove to everyone that it was indeed H. Jackson Brown Jr. who inspired my exploration, my dreams, and my soon discoveries. The rest of the questions were very trivial such as his favorite book, movie, quote etc… I had many more questions to ask but Ann yelled at me to turn off the light and go to sleep. I did as she requested and began making a nest on the floor to sleep in. She rejected and told me there was plenty of room on the bed with her. I stood there awkwardly for a few seconds until she interjected.

"Blake, seriously, grow up. I'm not gonna bite you or try to make a move. I'm tired and I just want to sleep." I nodded and made my way to the left side of the bed. I covered myself and closed my eyes and tried to doze off. It took much longer than it should have considering my exhaustion, but eventually I did succumb to sleep's welcoming hands to the gentle sound of Ann's soft breathing.

I had a weird dream/nightmare that night. I awoke in my room back home in an empty bed. I was undressed and vulnerable, so I made my way to my closet to find my clothes. As I opened my closet, I was thrown to find it empty. I quickly ran to my dresser, and that too was empty. All of my clothes were missing, and I couldn't find anything to cover myself with. I tried to grab my curtain but was unable to pull it. It felt like concrete. I tried to pull it down, but it refused to budge, so I gave up. I crept downstairs so as to not wake anybody. I was confused on where Ann went, and I decided to try and find her.

As I looked around my house, I noticed that everything seemed very off. The pictures on the wall, looked like they were out of place and the people in the pictures didn't seem recognizable. I shook off the uneasy feeling because I knew this was my house. I was certain this was where I was, but I was uncertain if this was where I needed to be. I continued to look, but was unable to find Ann, so I opened the front door and walked outside. I understood that I was unclothed, but I figured it was more important to find Ann, although I was unsure why.

The day was neither cool nor warm, it was neither dark nor light, it just was. I stepped off the porch and expected to feel my foot hit the ground, but I could not. I looked down and saw that the ground existed, and it held me up, however I could not feel it. I decided to not let it worry me and I continued on my path. The streets were empty. There were no cars and no pedestrians, it was just me. The park across the street stood clean and well-kept by invisible entities. I could hear the creaking of the swings, but I could feel no wind. However, eerie it might have been, I did not allow the chill to creep in through my spine. I breathed in and out slowly, as I trudged along. Step by step I made my way down the street towards the familiar tree towering above a humble faded blue house. The intense feeling of solitude shattered as I heard screaming from inside the house. I walked forward, like I was going to do something about it. My hands clenched into fists and I furrowed my eyebrows. I had never been in a fight before, but I imagined that was how they started. As I took my determined step toward the noise, the screaming came from behind me all of a sudden. I quickly spun around and saw a tall man wearing a military uniform. He looked familiar, but I didn't know how I knew him. I slowly approached him, and his face started to melt away to become unrecognizable. No sound would escape my lips as I attempted to make contact. Instead of me saying something, the man in the military uniform opened his mouth to speak. "If it's not a beautiful morning, let your cheerfulness make it one." He spoke in a very quiet and monotone voice and as he finished the 1237th instruction from *Life's Little Instruction Book*, his mouth appeared and smiled. This allowed the eerie feeling to finally wash over me like a tidal wave. Suddenly, I was drowning in my own self-doubt. As the man reached out to grab me, I screamed and woke up.

I was back in the motel with Ann and I was fully clothed. I lay there in the bed very conscientious of my excessive sweating and hoping to God that Ann was asleep and unbothered. I looked over at the clock on the night stand and it said 6:37 A.M. This time, I knew what had woken me and it was the faceless foe and the earnest search for Ann. I did a few breathing exercises to calm myself down and fruitlessly willed myself to go back to sleep. I continued to lay there listening to the sound of not only me breathing but her breathing as well. She snored, and I sniffled simultaneously as we audibly became one. We inhaled together, and we exhaled together slowly, wafting back towards the silent home of sleep. Eventually, I could only hear myself breathe as if she was no longer there and I allowed myself to be immersed once more in a deep slumber.

I woke up early in the morning ready to take on this day that I had been waiting for. This would finally be the day when I got to meet the author of my favorite quote. I was ready for this to be the first day of the rest of my life. The day I finally decided to heed Brown's advice. The day I would begin to explore, continue to dream, and start discovering. As I laid in bed prepared to take a shower and get dressed for the day, Ann began to stir next to me. I tensed up and felt myself check the smell of my breath like a juvenile. "Are you ready for this day, Blake? This is going to be the first day of the rest of your life." I nodded and smiled at her.

"What?" she asked.

"I just can't believe this is finally going to happen."

"Dang, Blake, you need to smile more often. You aren't half bad looking when you smile at me like that."

"You aren't half bad yourself, Ann." She looked at me and smiled. Having just exhausted my extensive amount of charming lines, we stood there awkwardly. She looked me up and down and I could have sworn she was checking me out.

"Alright, Romeo, go ahead and shower. It's a good thing we bought you some nice clothes at Wal-Mart."

After I finished my shower in record time, Ann and I checked out and made our way towards the Catoosa Creamery. We arrived a few minutes before the scheduled meeting because I needed to be punctual. Apparently, punctuality is something Rosemary is passionate about as well, because I immediately recognized her car from yesterday, parked in front of the store. I turned to Ann and smiled.

"Are you sure you are ready, Blake?"

"Absolutely," I responded. "I'm a little nervous, but it isn't anything I can't handle. I'm really excited about this, Ann. I also don't want you to think that I'm being rude if I ask you to not go in with me." I felt horrible for asking, but I didn't feel comfortable for some reason having Ann in the creamery with me as I talk with Rosemary. However, Ann seemed to understand this already and smiled.

"I get it, Blake. Now, go in there and figure out what you can about that quote!" I nodded and opened the driver's side door to get out of the Intrepid.

The days that I spent driving to Nashville was nothing compared to the distance from my car to the entrance of the Catoosa Creamery. It was only a few yards away, but it seemed like hundreds of miles with my mind wandering at warp speed. Would she actually tell me about the quote? Would she have brought her husband along? Would *he* tell me about the quote? Finally, after years of walking, I made it to the entrance of the shop. I was immediately surrounded by the smell of sweet dairy and ice cream. I looked frantically around the store for Rosemary and eventually spotted her in a corner booth reading a book. She saw me, put her book down, and smiled.

"Start meetings on time, regardless of who's missing," she said, quoting Brown's 398th instruction. "However, if I started this meeting without you, they might have locked me up in the loony bin for talking to myself. I'm glad you're on time." She stood up and hugged me and I hugged her back. We both ordered a chocolate milkshake and sat down. I started the conversation.

"How long have you and Mr. Brown lived here?"

"Oh, you can call him Harry. That's what I call him. Unless he's in trouble then it's Harriett." She laughed and continued. "We've been here for about 20 years actually."

"Oh, that's amazing! It's so pretty here."

"Yeah, we like it here. His publisher is over in Nashville, but Nashville isn't nearly as beautiful as it is here. So, when we need to, we'll make the drive over to Nashville and see even more of this gorgeous state. It's like a little mini vacation from our permanent vacation here. You're from Middleton correct?"

I nodded. I was surprised she remembered that small fact about me.

"So, you're a big fan of Harry's work?"

Again, I nodded. I probably looked really stupid.

"He'll be glad to know that someone is still paying attention to the stuff that he writes. Although, I don't think he writes for anyone else other than his family and himself. I think that might be what is charming about it. It's incredibly personal and people find that attractive, not just in writing you know." She winked. It was the same type of wink that an old person does after they know they just gave you sage words of wisdom.

"I just find everything that he writes to be real. It's all incredibly relatable and it gives off a pleasant feeling while you read it. I don't know, I guess that's probably because it's personal." Finally, I said something and only sounded a little stupid. Turns out I wasn't going to make a complete fool out of myself. Our milkshakes were delivered to our table and Rosemary's eyes lit up at the sight of hers. She began sipping immediately. I, however, was too anxious to touch mine. Only after she supped up half of her milkshake did she speak again.

"So, you had mentioned when we set up this little meeting that you had questions...inquiries? I can try my best to maybe give you the answers you are looking for."

"Uhmm...yeah. I...uh...wow this sounds really lame if I say it out loud."

Observation: Whenever one looks forward to something so much, they are unable to perform when this time comes.

Analysis: This is probably why your senior prom turns out to be disappointing. Or walking across the stage at graduation is unexciting. Or your first time having sex is quick and underwhelming. It's because you build it up in your head too much and it soon becomes less than expected and instead is humdrum.

Further Analysis: Sex is most definitely not the same thing as a conversation, but you get the concept.

Conclusion: Don't build something up in your head if you want to successfully follow through with it.

Rosemary waved me back to earth. "It won't sound lame."

"Okay," I agreed. "There is this certain quote that your husband is credited for that I love. It has kinda become my life motto recently. Anyway, Mark Twain was also credited for the same quote and I don't like Twain that much, so I don't want to like his quote. Does that make sense?"

She smiled and nodded. "It does make sense, dearie. However, I think I've failed to spot the question."

"I guess my question is did he actually say the quote or was it Mark Twain?"

"I assume you're talking about his quote that talks about looking back on your life twenty years from now, yes?"

I nodded. Finally, after all this time, after all those miles, after all that anticipation, my question was heard by someone who could answer it.

"I don't think I can answer that question for you, love."

Welp. Never mind.

"Harry has said many wonderful things in his lifetime that have not received any credit. As have many other people in this world. If Harry were here he would probably say something like: 'It's not the person that is an inspiration, but the person who has heard the quote and interpreted it for themselves.' In fact, he tells something along those lines to his grandchildren."

"Oh. Okay." I was defeated. My shoulders slumped back, and my head fell a little towards my shoulders. I scooted back from the edge of my seat and began messing with the straw of my untouched milkshake.

"I'll tell you what, sweetie. If you are not busy, I would love to have an extra hand at the farm where Harry and I live. He is making a solo trip to Nashville for a few days and I'll be needing as much help as I can outside with the few animals we have and tidying the place up. I'll pay you for each of your days helping and I won't keep you more than three days at the most. I'll be able to give you about two hundred dollars a day if you help me. Maybe you'll find your inspiration there."

I was speechless at first. For one, I didn't know what to do with Ann while I was helping Rosemary. For another, I would be able to be in Brown's residence for a considerable amount of time and like Rosemary said, I could find my new inspiration there. "I definitely don't want to impose on your living situation," I said respectfully. Of course, I wanted to do this, but I had to reject first as it was the polite thing to do. I waited a half a second to hear Rosemary say what I knew she would.

"It wouldn't be an imposition for me at all. How could extra hands on the farm become a burden?"

I smiled and so did Rosemary. We knew we had come to an agreement. I stood up and shook her hand a little too eagerly.

"I'll write down the address and I'm sure you can find your way just fine. I'll be expecting to see you tomorrow morning bright and early." She finished up the second half of her milkshake in one continuous drink, handed me a napkin with the address, and gave me a hug as she made her way out of the shop. I held the napkin in my hand and just stared at it in amazement. I couldn't believe this was happening. If I couldn't learn the origins of the quote, maybe I could live some of the quotes with the author himself, or maybe his wife at least. I was ready to throw my bowlines and make my way to the Brown's farm to help out in any way I could. I sat there with excitement as I slurped up my entire milkshake. I could have given Rosemary a run for her money.

I made my way back to the Intrepid, with my napkin in hand. I was glowing as I sat back in the driver seat.

"Well aren't you happy. I'm assuming the meeting went well?" Ann said eager to hear the spoiler to the mystery of the quote. "So, who was it?"

"Actually," I started. "I didn't find out." Ann's face dropped a little.

"Well that sucks. But something good did come from this meeting, yes? I walked around this little plaza due to boredom, so I want to hear that I didn't do it for nothing."

"Actually, the meeting went really well. Rosemary actually offered me a job." Ann looked confused and a little angry.

"Wait, what? You can't take a job right now. We need to go back to Middleton at some point. As much as I would love to drive away and never look back it wouldn't be fair to *your* mom."

I looked over at her. "Or your mom and dad, right?" She didn't answer, and I felt her tense up a little bit. "Besides," I continued, reaching out for her arm, "it's only for a few days, three at the most. I'll just be helping out at their farm." I held up my first two fingers on my left hand and held my right hand to my heart, "scouts honor."

Ann laughed. "That means nothing, you weren't even a scout. Except for that day that you were a girl scout."

This time, I laughed. "That was only because you made me go to that stupid party with you, so you could trick the other girls in your troop into thinking you had a boyfriend."

"Hey," she stated. "It was a big deal if you had a boyfriend in the 5th grade. Especially if it lasted as long as ours did."

I rolled my eyes. "I can't believe our imaginary 3 weeks was a momentous accomplishment as 5th graders. They were a pretty kick ass imaginary 3 weeks though," She smiled and agreed. She stared at me for a quiet moment. I spoke again to bring us back on topic.

"Anyways, I don't want to ditch you for three days."

"Don't worry, Blake, I'll be fine. I have aunt that lives around here that I can probably stay with." She seemed a little defeated but tried her best to hide it.

"Are you kidding me!? Why the hell did we pay to sleep in a hotel if you had an aunt that we could have crashed with?"

"Oh, come on. That would not have been as exciting or adventurous. That's called pulling in the bowlines and sailing towards the safe harbor," she taunted.

"Okay fine, I guess we can't go back and change it. I just want to make sure you'll be okay while I am gone for three days."

"Of course, I will be okay. I would, however, like to hear how each of your days go. Do you want to meet up each evening and reconvene?"

"That would be great. We can just come back to the creamery," I suggested.

"Sounds like a plan. I can call my aunt and have her pick us up if you want to sleep there tonight before heading to the farm tomorrow."

"Nah, let's spend another night in the hotel. Besides, with the money Rosemary is giving me, I'll be able to pay back everything on my credit card from the past few days and then some. Tonight, we splurge."

Note: Something did happen that night between Ann and me.

After

"How are you doing, honey?" My mom posed the question extremely cautiously. I mean, she knew I was incredibly upset, but she also knew that there wasn't really anything that she could do about all of it.

"I'm hanging in there, Mom. I really appreciate everything you've been doing for me, and I love you very much." She smiled at that. I don't tell my mom I love her every day, and while I regret that, I really appreciate it when she smiles so widely when I do say it. I would be heartbroken if she began to expect it or if it did not make as much of an impact on her.

Before

We got back to the hotel room later that afternoon. We had walked around the Catoosa Creamery plaza a little bit before we left, which killed some time. Instead of going to sleep immediately, or turning on the TV, Ann laid on the bed and motioned for me to sit next to her. I did as she suggested, and we were both lying next to each other and lying to each other about what all of this meant. I didn't bring it up, however. She shifted around until I found her laying on her side, looking at me.

"What?" I asked.

"I just keep trying to figure you out, Blake. We've been friends for years and years and I'm still not quite there yet."

I smiled. "Good luck. I still haven't figured myself out." We laid there for a few moments more. The only noise in the room was the sound of our soft breaths slowly synching up together and the incredibly loud pounding of my heart which I hoped only I could hear.

"Do you remember when we first met?" she said, creating a gentle opening in the quiet room.

"Of course, I do. It's that typical girl next door story. I was sitting in my room playing video games when I saw the moving van from my window. At first, I was annoyed because you guys were making a lot of noise. However, when I saw you get out I thought to myself, 'Oh cool, someone my age to play with.' This was, of course, when girls still had cooties."

Ann snorted. "Oh naturally, so, my mom made me knock on your door to see if you guys had a moving dolly because, of course, the van we rented didn't have one."

"Oh yeah, I answered the door and thought you were crazy. Who the heck has one of those things? My mom and dad came to the door to meet you and were stoked to find out we were in the same 5th grade class in August."

"I think it was just your dad at the door. Anyway, I was pretty excited too," Ann said. "Plus, girls never really have a 'boys have cooties' phase. Or, at least, I didn't. I thought you were cute and I was excited to have a cute boy in my class." My heart became a presumptuous pianist's pounding metronome set a little too fast.

"But, we grew up," I said. "and that sucks."

"But, we grew up together, and that didn't suck," she smiled.

"Wow, what a poet you are, Ann. 'That didn't suck.'" She laughed and inched towards me a little bit. My inner metronome sped up about 60 beats per minute.

"So, we grew up. We got smarter and we got closer. Yes?"

I responded to her statement very quietly. "Not close enough." She smiled again so I added a little bit more. "We still have time together though, we can be closer." This time, she did not smile. Instead, she frowned and inched away.

"I wish it could be that easy, Blake."

"Why can't it?" I said a little forcefully. My face tilted like a confused dog while my eyes longed for the answer. I continued. "I don't understand. Why can't it? We've been friends for years and years and I've had to watch us grow so close but feeling ever more distant. What are we working towards here? I just don't understand and I'm not sure what to do anymore." We just laid there for a few moments. Her not knowing what to say and I driving the same boat. I thought of a poem that I had read one time. I couldn't remember the author, but it was incredibly powerful. As I thought about the poem, I altered it for mine and Ann's sake.

"At one time, I was a child upset with summer's lateness and the impending autumn season bringing with it the dreaded days in the halls and classrooms. But then I grew up.

At one time, I was a first grader, upset with school's longevity and the looming educational career ahead of me. But then I grew up.

At one time, I was a child upset with summer's lateness yet again and awaiting those days in the classrooms and hallways. But then I grew up.

At one time, I was a child, upset with the fence in my yard prohibiting my ability to see the moving van pull into the house down the street. But then I grew up.

At one time, I was a fifth grader, upset with my shyness to talk to the girl who asked me for help in the impending autumn air. But then I grew up.

At one time we were children upset with the sun for going down too soon in those summer evenings forcing us to part ways for the day. But then we grew up.

At one time, we were sixth graders, upset with the school bell signaling the end of lunch and forcing us to part ways for the afternoon. But then we grew up.

At one time, we were children upset with age and time wanting to stay young and together. But everyone grows up.

At one time, I was a Sophomore upset with the hierarchy of high school and longing for those short summer nights with you. But I knew you grew up.

At one time, we were Seniors, upset with each other for not making enough of an effort to rekindle a long-lost friendship. But then we grew up.

At one time, we will be adults upset with ourselves for losing someone so close to us and allowing them to become a distant memory and wanting to do something about it. Instead, we will grow up.

At one time, we will no longer grow up and we will have lost something dear to us.

At one time, we will no longer grow up and we will become another pair of footprints who had attempted to make an impact on humanity but instead we become a pair of memories.

Why?

Because everyone grows up."

Again, I wasn't quite sure who the author of the poem was, but it was close to how I was feeling as I silently laid in the hotel bed next to Ann. We were growing up and it was terrible. I didn't understand why it had to happen and I didn't understand why I wouldn't do something about it. I thought of another quote about growing up by the Russian novelist, Fyodor Dostoyevsky, in his short story called, *Notes from the Underground.*

Dostoyevsky writes, "For, after all, you do grow up, you do outgrow your ideals, which turn to dust and ashes, which are shattered into fragments; and if you have no other life, you just have to build one up from these fragments. And all the time your soul is craving and longing for something else. And in vain does the dreamer rummage about in his old dreams, raking them over as though they were a heap of cinders, looking in these cinders for some spark, however tiny, to fan it into a flame so as to warm his chilled blood by it and revive in it all that he held dear before, all that touched his heart, that made his blood course through his veins, that drew tears from his eyes, and that so splendidly deceived him."

This is a very pessimistic quote however true or untrue it may be. Dostoyevsky believes all ambitions to be fragile enough to "shatter into fragments." I can't quite decide if I agree with this or not. I do know that dreams and ambitions are incredibly powerful. They are strong enough to motivate the human populous to do almost anything. Dreams and the imagination are strong enough to break any personal limitation or self-doubt. If this is the case, if dreams could do these things, then how can they be so fragile as to break into a million pieces? The Russian novelist also seems to think that the dreams deceived him at the end of his quote. Again, I would argue that they only become deceptive if they are not turned into a reality. Anyone would become disappointed if they relied so much on something and it was whisked away from them. People all have a dream that they strive towards and are disenchanted when they become unattainable, thus making the dreams devilish and deceptive. This is when I understood.

I thought about all of this in those silent moments with Ann. She did not speak, and neither did I as I tried to sort through all the thoughts that raced around in my head in those quick flashes of time. I managed to compile all those thoughts into a sentence that I successfully said out loud. "Pluck the day."

She looked at me curiously. "Why is our Roman friend getting brought back up?"

"It always comes back to this. It comes back to 'fleeting time' and our constant fear of it. It always comes back to having no regrets and living now because we don't know what is going to happen next. We don't know who we might lose tomorrow or the day after. We can never know these things. So, we have to heed Horace's warning." I stopped myself before I went further, but Ann pushed me.

"So, heed his advice, Blake." She inched towards me again and my heart picked up its quickening tempo. I thought of Ann's first knock on my door. I thought of the first time I saw her smiling face. I thought of our days in school. I thought about her holding my hand for the first time as she beckoned me to follow her to a playground. I thought of her laugher and looked at her smile. I thought of the warmth of her breath as she lay next to me. I thought about the beauty that was Ann Paige. I thought of her majestic being and I heeded his advice.

"I love you, Ann Paige. I love you. You are strong and willing, but you are also fragile and reserved. You are my dream, Ann Paige. You are everything that my soul is craving and longing for. I have held onto you, unwilling to let you fall and shatter into fragments because I don't know what I would do without you. You are the dream I am afraid will disappoint me. You are the dream I am afraid will deceive me, but I cannot continue to let my fear slow me down as time is speeding up. I love you and I love that you are my dream. I want to explore with you and I want to discover a life with you. I want my dream to dream with me as we heed Brown's advice together." I laid there quietly again as Ann just looked at me. Everything I said obviously did not surprise her, how could it? Eventually she spoke.

"Dostoyevsky was sort of overrated if you ask me. A little too morbid and depressed." She sat there in silence again.

"Is that all you have to say!?" is what I *wanted* to say. "Maybe a little too sad," is what I *actually* said. We sat there in silence again. This time, I could not break the stillness, it had to be her. It was.

"I love you too, Blake. Of course, I do." I felt a sudden burst of relief hit me all at once as though I had finally made it up for air after being underwater for too long. "You didn't pay enough attention to the beginning of Dostoyevsky's quote though. He says, 'you do grow up, you do outgrow your ideals, which turn to dust and ashes…'" I felt myself get forced back underwater. "I am turning to dust and ashes, Blake. I can't be around anymore. You are growing up. I am growing up. We can't grow up together." I felt myself 'rummaging about' looking for 'some spark to fan it into a fame so as to warm my chilled body.' I was so lost suddenly and confused. She continued because she didn't know the damage she had already caused. "When we get back home, we can't continue to pretend that we are school kids again. We need to begin to go our separate ways, so we don't hold each other back. I don't need to hold you back, Blake. You need to be able to explore the world, dream of things better than me, and discover things you never would have imagined, and I can't do any of that with you. I love you enough to hold onto what we have now and for the next few days. I love you enough to let that all go when we get back. I love you enough to let you go when we get back. I love you enough that our tale becomes tragic. Can you love me the same?"

I didn't say anything. How could I? She seemed to understand however, as she closed her eyes and quickly drifted off to sleep. Or at least it looked as though she did. I however, was not as lucky. I spent most of that night staring up at the ceiling and trying to hold onto my dream. It felt as though I were a little kid holding onto an action figure as I started to doze off. Whenever this happened I would wake up to the sound of my toy hitting the floor as I was unable to hold onto anything when my body fell asleep. In the hotel room, I continued to hold onto my dream as I started to find my way into the relaxing darkness. However, now that I had grown up, I did not wake up to the sound of my failure as my dream dropped and shattered into fragments. *I guess dreams are fragile after all.*

Speaking of dreams: I awoke again in my room back home in the same empty bed as last time. I was still undressed and still vulnerable. This dream began to play out much like the one the previous night.

I made my way to my closet to find my clothes and again found it to be completely empty. All my clothes were missing still, and my curtains remained immovable. I continued downstairs and was greeted with the familiar urge to find where Ann had gone. The pictures on the wall were once more out of place and unrecognizable. I continued to look for Ann but was unable to find her. I opened the front door and walked outside, this time prepared for the nonexistent climate. The day was continually neither cool nor warm, it was neither dark nor light, it just was. The park across the street continued to stand clean and well-kept by invisible entities. Step by step I made my way down the street towards the familiar tree towering above a humble faded blue house. The intense feeling of solitude shattered again as I heard screaming from inside the house. I walked forward, like I was going to do something about it. As I took my step, the screaming came from behind me suddenly. I quickly spun around and saw the tall familiar man wearing the military uniform. I approached him, and his face started to melt away to become unrecognizable yet again. No sound would escape my lips as I attempted to make contact. Instead, the man in the military uniform opened his mouth to speak. "Never miss an opportunity to go fishing with your father." He spoke in a very quiet and monotone voice and as he finished the 1260th instruction from *Life's Little Instruction Book*, his mouth appeared and smiled. I was again drowning in my own self-doubt. As the man reached out to grab me, I screamed. He grabbed my shoulder and pulled me closer to him. His face began to reform into the shape of my father's face. I was never afraid of my father when I was younger, and I am still unafraid. However, in that situation, my father's face was incredibly frightening and off putting. I tried to shake his arm off me and run away but I was unable. I continued to scream and eventually woke up to the quiet darkness of the hotel room.

Seven

Before

I looked at my clock and it was 6:37 A.M. This time, I knew what had awakened me and I was not eager to continue thinking about it. I looked over at the other side of the bed, but it was empty. I guess Ann had already gotten up and left for her aunt's house. I rolled my eyes and gathered my stuff to head to the address that Rosemary had given to me.

I hoped I'd arrived on time. Rosemary and I had not agreed on a set time other than, "bright and early." I looked up at the sky and it was bright. I looked down at my watch and it was early...relatively. I pulled my car up the vast driveway until I reached the cul de sac that was stationed in front of the house. I parked my car behind an older pickup truck that obviously belonged to Mr.

Brown. As I got out I was taken aback by how moderate their house was. I fully expected the house to be incredibly spacious and full at the same time. I expected to see garden gnomes and flowers loudly placed in the front yard. I expected there to be decorations hanging from the banisters on the porch. This was not the case. In fact, the massive amount of farmland loomed over the quaint two-story homestead. I wasn't quite sure what to bring to this "job," so I packed pretty much everything I owned at the time which could be easily carried in a Wal-Mart bag. I closed my car door as I pulled out my makeshift luggage and took a deep breath in an attempt to compose myself. Eventually, I knew it was finally time for me to walk up to the front door and knock. Knock. Knock. Knock. I waited. Nothing. Knock. Knock. Knock. After a few more seconds of silence, I finally heard hurried footsteps approaching the door. It opened with enthusiasm as she said, "I'm so glad you're here even though you're late." I laughed. Even though the Browns no longer lived as geographically south as they once did, it appears they remained with that southern charm.

I spoke while she made her way towards the back of the house. "Well, just so we are on the same page, what time would you like me ready in the morning?"

She laughed this time as she opened the gate to her fenced in backyard. She walked towards a small garden, kneeled down and said, "I think I made it pretty clear, my dear. You came when it was bright, but you weren't here when it was early." She started to tend to her garden humming, what sounded like an old church hymn that I recognized, quietly to herself. I knelt next to her and quietly sang along.

> "I come to the garden alone,
> While the dew is still on the roses,
> And the voice I hear falling on my ear
> The Son of God discloses.
> And He walks with me, and He talks with me,
> And He tells me I am His own;
> And the joy we share as we tarry there,
> None other has ever known."

We worked there in that garden for a little while, Rosemary and me. We worked without gloves because it connected us more that way. Without gloves we were able to work together and were able to connect with God and nature. We were content. At one point, Rosemary got up to make us lemonade and I was alone in that garden for a short time. I continued to tend to the soil and carefully planted my tomato seeds in their newly made bed.

I'd never gardened in my life. For the first little while in the garden, I just watched Rosemary move about with gentle fluidity. I tried to learn what I could and eventually tried my hand at it. I was so caught up in my work that I became ignorant to Rosemary's absence. I finished planting the last little bit of seeds, covered them with a little soil, and gently watered them. Gently. That is what seemed like the key to gardening as far as I could tell. I then stood up and looked at my completed work. For what seemed like the first time in my life, I had made something, and I was proud of it. I'm not talking about a 5th grade science fair project or a plate of spaghetti. I mean something that is alive, and something that can flourish. I was proud of my hopeful handiwork. I was probably more proud or impressed by the tools that were at my disposal. That was nothing I could control, and I was grateful that God gave me two hands to use, seeds to plant, and water to help them grow. I was, for a few moments, at peace with God, the world, and those soon to be tomatoes. More so, however, I was at peace with myself; and it was nice. It was very nice.

"Remember that children, marriages, and flower gardens reflect the kind of care they get." I heard Rosemary quote her husband as she came out not long after the tomato seeds were finished being planted. "I reckon you found a new passion, my dear." I smiled and took the glass of lemonade she was handing me.

"I'd reckon you are right. That was very peaceful and spiritual." I took a sip and sighed.

"Nothing beats freshly squeezed lemonade," I added. Rosemary smiled.

"There ain't ever been nothin' wrong with gettin' spiritual with the Lord. Let's go inside and get you settled into the guest room. I'd help you with your bags, but it looks like you've only got one. Is it full of groceries?" I grabbed the said bag from the back porch where it was haphazardly tossed prior to my spiritual experience in the garden and followed Rosemary into the house.

The back door led us directly into the kitchen that seemed very spacious due to the large window overlooking the backyard and the aforementioned garden. In the middle of the kitchen rested a long island which was home to the deep kitchen sink. The top of the island was a darker wood countertop. It gave the kitchen a very "homey" feeling. However, the island was also home to the stainless-steel stove top which made me uncomfortable considering all the wood. The bottom of the island consisted of storage and was a creamy white color that matched the rest of the cabinets and the window pane. Two hanging lights found themselves overlooking the island which helped to brighten the already bright room due to the large window's natural light. There were also three old wooden beams that rested on the ceiling which I doubted and hoped were not part of the structural integrity of the house. We then made our way through the kitchen and into the living room. The first thing I noticed about the living room was the lack of a television. Since the world is a few years into the 21st century, it feels like a television or some kind of entertainment device is a necessity for a living room. However, Rosemary and Mr. Brown had decorated the space so well, that it seems complete even in the 21st century. The modern, rustic, living room was fitted with two rocking chairs and a couch. It seemed, just like the kitchen, like the room was a southern cliché which ranged from red and white plaid blankets to a wooden fireplace. Rosemary walked over and fluffed the pillows on the couch.

"It's just a habit." She said. There was not a centered light in the room but large windows again that paralleled the natural light of the kitchen. For the night time, only two lamps and a fireplace would bring light into the room and this seemed like enough. We made our way upstairs and everything was as equally homey. Their house was as far from tiny as it was far from huge. It was a perfect contrast of humble yet comfortable.

"You can go right ahead and put your groceries down on the bed." I nodded and plopped my bag of non-groceries on the foot of the bed. "Very good, now why don't I show you around the farm a little bit and you can start to make yourself at home."

I smiled. "I don't feel like that will be very hard. Your house is beautiful and very welcoming."

"I appreciate you saying that, Blake. Let's go have a look around."

We found ourselves walking out the back porch again and I smiled when I eyed my nonexistent tomatoes. I think I hoped to have seen something happen in the 2 minutes since I finished my work. I followed Rosemary to the end of the yard and she pushed on the large picket fence towards the rest of the farm. My jaw dropped when I saw the land behind it.

"Put your tongue back in your mouth, love. Follow me." I did as she instructed. It was made apparent to me that Rosemary seemed much more comfortable at her house than at the Catoosa Creamery or at her unnecessary job at the convenience store. This was not a bad thing or a negative observation. In fact, I appreciated her comfortability with me. It makes me feel a lot less like we just met and that she was instead, a long lost relative. Rosemary was just as caring and just as loving, and I appreciated it greatly.

"Well, this is the farm. What do you think, hon?"

"It's huge." I said stupidly.

"Well, this is what Harry loves to do after he's done writin'."

"I don't blame him, it's breathtaking."

"Yeah, well these are our new stomping grounds and we are content with ourselves and at peace with God. Come now, lemme show you some of these animals Harry's got running 'round here."

I followed her some more over a small, dirt path to the group of stables down the field. "Do you grow anything here? It just looks like grass to me." I asked curiously.

Rosemary shook her head. "No, sir, that'll be too much work. We keep the grass cut as much as we can but mostly the cows graze it nice and short and the rest of the animals just enjoy running 'round the place. I think Harry's got all this place for them. He loves 'em a whole lot and so do I. How could you not?" I assumed I would understand as soon as we reached the stables.

However, she turned out to be right. The animals were magnificent.

First, we made our way to the barn to see the cows. I've of course seen cows before, but never this close. Rosemary instructed me that I was to help take them out of the barn and lead them to the field. I once read that cows can get really excited about being let into the field after long periods of confinement. The amazing part about that, is witnessing it firsthand. I watched as the large, spotted dogs quickly made their way into the field to start grazing. I stood there watching as Rosemary grabbed my shoulder and I knew it was time to follow her again.

We headed towards the horse stables after releasing the cows for grazing. While I thought how beautiful the spotted, dairy animals were, I knew the horses would surpass their beauty. The very moment I walked in and allowed my eyes to adjust to the shaded, indoor space, I was overcome with raw emotion. I saw about a dozen large eyes peering out from almost all the stalls. These dark-coated animals looked at me with a curiosity and a gentleness that felt welcoming.

"These are our prides of the farm. Harry loves these beauties almost as much as his own kiddos – myself included." Rosemary laughed and pulled up a stool to sit down. I continued to walk to each stall and visit with each of the curious pairs of eyes. As I made my way down, I noticed that I was approaching an empty stall. Rosemary continued while I finished my rounds. "All of them need a bit of love so as to remind them how beautiful they are. It helps their confidence," she added.

Finally, I made it to the empty stall and became the curious peering eyes. I saw a pearl white horse lazily chewing on hay in the back of the stall. It seemed to sense me because it turned around and looked at me. This look was not a look of curiosity, but a look of acknowledgement. I felt Rosemary's hand on my shoulder as she started to speak.

"This one, however, she doesn't require any special attention. She seems to already know how beautiful she is. She doesn't seem to try, she's just confident and comfortable in her own skin." She smiled and stared at the magnificent creature. "Even when all the others go out on the pasture, Belle sticks by herself across the ways. She doesn't need our attention or the others'." I continued to stare at Belle, desperate for her to acknowledge me again. She didn't stare back.

"Come on, we'll leave her alone for a little while. I'll show you the rest of the farm and see if we can find some more animals to show you. We'll see if you find a favorite and we'll get you set up to work with them for the next few days."

Observation: The animals on the Brown's farm were beyond beautiful.

Analysis on Observation: The horses were by far the most beautiful of the animals.

Continued Analysis on Observation: There should not be a stigma attached to my interest in horses. They're awesome

Conclusion: Horses are awesome.

The tour lasted longer than I thought it would. Most likely because of the vast size of the Brown's land. After showing me the horses, Rosemary and I rode on a golf cart while she showed me the rest of the animals, which included goats and pigs. She also showed me a variety of different flowers that had been growing. I figured that Rosemary felt as much passion for the flowers as Mr. Brown felt for the animals and that I could feel for those horses. It was a beautiful life they had built for themselves: surrounded by their love for each other and surrounded by their love for the outdoors.

When we finally made it back up to the house, I noticed the cows had been put away and there were some farm hands cleaning up after them. For some reason it surprised me to see helpers but after adding some logic to my thoughts, it made sense. Rosemary and Mr. Brown were too old to tend to the farm by themselves. In fact, it seemed like they were too old to even walk around the land without a little help from a golf cart. However, I was confused as to why Rosemary asked me here to help if she already had a group of experienced helpers. I decided to ask.

"Why did you hire me if you already have abled bodies around?"

Rosemary smiled and said, "That doesn't mean I still don't need you here. That also doesn't mean you don't need to be here." I quickly started to realize at that point that Rosemary didn't really need my help. She was doing me a favor.

We listened to the birds chirp and sing as we made our way back towards the house, leaving the golf cart with the cows in the barn. I looked up to see the different birds flying in their own different directions, each of them on a mission. I wondered if they looked down on Rosemary and me, curious of our quest. If they did, they were not curious long. They continued to fly away in all different directions. Interesting enough, while the chaotic birds continued to disperse, a flock of geese flew into the middle forming a tight V-formation. These geese brought organization to the unorganized.

"Do you know why one of the sides of the 'V' is longer than the other?" Rosemary asked, noticing my strange infatuation with the geese.

"No, why?" I inquired. She stopped leading us and turned towards me as if she were going to tell me a secret.

Finally, she said, "There are more geese on that side." I laughed as I was whisked back to reality and away from my metaphorical thoughts. We giggled the rest of the way back to the quaint house.

We settled back into the house and made our way into the living room and talked.

"So, what would you like to do around here for the next few days?" She asked me simply. I didn't answer because I didn't want to intrude. So, she spoke again. "If I had my druthers, I'd keep you indoors with me: cookin', cleanin', and chattin'. However, I know you want to be outside."

"It seems to me like you already have a place in mind for me, ma'am."

"Well, Harry usually works with the horses, so we don't have anybody to be with them until he gets back. It seemed to me like you enjoyed their company. Is that a safe bet?"

"Yes, ma'am. I liked them very much."

"Well, alright. I'll have Zeke show you what to do as soon as we eat some lunch."

Rosemary made us some simple salads, using garden fresh cucumbers that she picked that morning and some homemade salad dressing. It was nice to sit and talk with her about school and back home. She didn't ask how my trip was and she didn't ask about Ann. It was a breath of fresh air and I was as happy as when I planted those tomatoes.

After we finished eating, Rosemary promised to do my dishes for me and I made my way to the horse stables to meet Zeke. Zeke was one of the farm hands who helped with the horses and other animals. He was a normal looking guy who didn't seem to be dressed for farm work. He was wearing khakis, converse high tops, and a red hoodie. For some reason, I was expecting to see boots, jeans, and a flannel. (I think my assumption is justified). Despite his appearance, Zeke seemed to really know what he was doing, and I immediately learned a lot. Basically, however, my job was to show the horses attention by brushing them and cleaning up their pens. He said that it may be gross, but it was better than it sounded. He also let me know that he would be around to help in case I needed anything. This made me feel better.

"Besides just showing them attention and cleaning up, we'll take them out for a few hours each day and let them stretch out and play. It's not a good idea to keep them in here too long because they'll get anxious and uncomfortable. The Brown's want their animals to enjoy being here. So, we help in whatever way we can." This seemed admirable. "Since you are only here for the rest of today, tomorrow, and a short while the day after, I won't get too complicated with specifics. All you really need to know is a bit about these horses and how they act." Zeke then proceeded to tell me all about the Brown's horses including their different breeds and some of their attitudes.

The Brown's own a few different breeds of horses including: two Tennessee Walking Horses, four Quarter Horses, and a French Camargue. The Camargue was already my favorite. According to Zeke, the French Camargue is born black and becomes pearl white as it grows up. They live to be about 25 and are supposedly really gentle. Because of their easy temperament, they are kind of lone wolves. This would explain Belle's attitude this morning. Camargues also are supposed to have remarkable stamina. They can go on a long spontaneous journey and not grow tired. Needless to say, I was looking forward to spending the next few days with Belle. Despite her cold attitude, my stubbornness drove me to try to get to know her.

For the rest of the day, Zeke and I worked on cleaning up the individual boxes. While we did this, we let all seven of the equine roam around. Eventually, Zeke went home, and Rosemary called me in for dinner. After the day that I had had with Rosemary, I expected an exceedingly cliché country cuisine. However, when I entered the kitchen I smelled a familiar dish and it was something that I had recently at the Hall's.

"How very country of you to be making pizza," I laughed.

"Oh, dear, I didn't make this. I got it delivered." She laughed alongside me as she pulled the delivery box out of the oven where it was keeping warm. I washed my hands at the sink and found myself sitting across from Rosemary at the kitchen table. She prayed a simple prayer over the food before we ate. "God is great, God is good, and we thank him for our food. Keep watch over us the next few days, Lord, and allow us to remember who you are. Amen."

When we started eating, I began to speak to Rosemary about my day with Zeke and Belle. "Zeke and I spent most of the day –"

She interrupted. "I'm sorry, love, I'm going to stop you right there. The dinner table is for pleasant conversation only. This means no business and no horse crap." She smiled and told me to continue with the edited version. I laughed and happily obliged. The conversation was great and perfectly stimulating. We ate until we were full, and we procrastinated doing the dishes until we absolutely had to.

Eight

Before

After finishing the dishes with Rosemary, I left to meet up with Ann at the creamery as promised. She was already in a booth with an ice cream cone in hand when I arrived. I waved at her through the window and she smiled when she saw me. I ordered a cookie dough ice cream cone and slid into the booth across from her. She had also ordered cookie dough and was the first to speak. "So," she said. "Tell me all about it!" So, I did. I spoke, and she listened. As I told her about the garden and the horses, I observed her listening to me. She listened so intensely. She listened as though she had heard this story a hundred times but didn't mind at all to hear it again. She greeted my story the way she greets me; like an old friend. I finished up my story as I told her about the "authentic country dinner." Ann, of course, laughed at Rosemary's choice of entrée and finished up her own dairy treat.

"Sounds like you had a successful day today."

"I did, it was incredible. How about you though? This debriefing is supposed to be a two-way street. How is your aunt?"

Ann shrugged. "Eh. She's fine. She got a new dog that she named Beauty. She is really sweet and lives up to her name. Other than that, nothing is really new with her."

"Well, that's good to hear, I guess," I said. I felt a little bad dominating the conversation, but there was so much to tell her, and she didn't seem to have a lot to tell me. In fact, after she told me about Beauty, we helplessly held onto small strands of conversation before its early death.

"Well, I should try and get back before Rosemary worries." I stood up and so did Ann.

"Yeah, no me too. I don't want to keep Aunt Sue waiting. I'll see you tomorrow? Same time?"

I hugged her and said, "Yes ma'am." She smiled, walked out the door, and that was that.

Only as I was driving back to the farm did I realize how forced the end of our meeting was. Up until I finished the retelling of my day, things went totally normal. She was listening, and I was happy to have her attention. However, when I asked about her day, things felt fake. I no longer felt like I was talking with Ann but instead was talking with someone who had stolen her face. What had I said that caused her to shut down on me?

I spent the rest of the drive shrugging off the encounter and eventually found myself in the quietly quaint farm house. I got undressed and laid down in the slightly uncomfortable bed. It felt as though no one had laid in it for a while. *Maybe I'm not the only one benefitting from the company for a few days,* I thought as I easily fell asleep with no nightmarish interruptions.

I woke up earlier than the day before, per Rosemary's request. I was eager to get started with the day, and I quickly ate the toast and eggs that Rosemary made for the both of us. Apparently, her country cuisine was back after our pizza last night because she offered me a bowl of grits to go along with my breakfast. I politely declined.

"Fair enough, then," she said as she ate some herself.

"What's on the docket for today?" I asked as I began to wash my plate.

"You'll have to ask Zeke about that. It will probably be similar to yesterday afternoon." I finished washing my plate, thanked Rosemary, and headed towards the stables.

Zeke was already there wearing his converse shoes, khakis, and a different hoodie.

"Howdy," I said mockingly.

He laughed and replied, "You ready to work?"

"Never," I joked.

Our work was incredibly similar to the work we did yesterday. We let the animals out to gallop and play while we cleaned up the stalls. I wish I could say that there was some excitement before lunch, but there was not. We finished cleaning right at lunch time, so I put the hose and rake away and headed up to the house to wash up. Zeke stayed behind because his brother, Marcus, was dropping off his lunch and he wanted to check on some of the livestock.

Zeke grew up in a comfortable home in Louisiana with his mom, step-dad, brother, and younger sister. He says he owes most of his comfort to his step-dad for opening up a healthy home for his mom and siblings. He also says that Hurricane Katrina, while a terrible tragedy, probably saved his family because that's how his mom met his step-dad. I didn't catch his parent's names. Eventually, his brother, Marcus, moved out to go to veterinary school and soon graduated and started a practice outside of the Catoosa Reserves. Zeke went with Marcus to go to school at Hiwassee College in Madisonville, Tennessee.

"I knew I definitely wanted to go to a smaller school and Hiwassee fit that criteria. Also, I liked that there was a degree in Christian studies." He told me.

"I didn't know you wanted to study religion?" I said as more of a question.

"Yeah, I'd love to find a job as a youth leader or something. That way, I can find kids who started out down a hard road like me and help them find a path."

"That's really honorable, is that what your step-dad did for you after the hurricane?"

"Yeah, I owe it to him to pay it forward."

According to Zeke, his younger sister, Tasha, is interested in music and wants to be a choir director. Both he and his brother want to do everything they can to help see it through with her.

After I finished washing my hands and as soon as I sat down to eat, Zeke ran up to the back door of the kitchen and began knocking furiously. Rosemary, already standing by the door opened it up and allowed Zeke to begin rambling. Now, I didn't catch every word that Zeke spouted, but I understood enough to figure out what was going on. As it turns out, the stubbornness of Belle wasn't the only reason for her reluctant movement, socializing, or appetite.

"My brother is going to do some blood work, but he believes her symptoms are linked to WEE." As Zeke said this, Rosemary looked defeated. He continued. "Marcus isolated Belle but is going to run the blood of all of the other horses just to make sure they didn't get infected." I was mostly confused.

"What is WEE?"

"It's called Western Equine Encephalitis. It's a virus that gets passed by mosquito bites. So, Belle can't infect the others, but there's no telling what mosquitos might've gotten to the other livestock." Rosemary continued to look sad as she listened to Zeke.

"Can we do anything?" I asked, thinking of Belle and her stubbornness.

"Marcus is going to treat her. He said the only reason he is worried is because of the timeframe. We don't know how long she's had these symptoms. It's hard, especially with Belle, because we aren't usually concerned due to her stubborn attitude."

"Thank you, Zeke. Please tell Marcus we are appreciative of his work and care." Zeke nodded his head towards Rosemary to acknowledge the kind words. He then took off back towards Marcus and the horses.

After that, Rosemary and I ate our lunch in silent thought.

Rosemary seemed reluctant about letting me go back with Zeke, Marcus, and Belle but approved after my own stubbornness. When I got back, Marcus was gone, and Zeke stood by Belle's stall.

"You know, she's always been my favorite one," he said as he saw me walking towards him. "I guess it's because she doesn't show me the time of day. Is that weird?"

I smiled and said, "Nah, girls will do that to you, too. I guess animals can do the same." Zeke looked puzzled.

He laughed and said, "Are you saying girls are animals?"

"Whoa!" I said quickly putting up my hands in defense. "Don't put words in my mouth. Rosemary might hear you and slap me across the head."

Marcus chuckled as he agreed. "You got that right."

There wasn't much that Zeke and I could do besides sit with Belle. We had let the other horses out of their stalls to run off the stress of having their blood drawn. Zeke said Marcus weren't wasting any time with the blood work and hoped to have it back by the end of the day or early tomorrow morning. So, we waited, and we cleaned. Eventually, Rosemary came to sit with Belle while Zeke and I finished up some chores. There wasn't much conversation to be had while we kept ourselves busy. I took advantage of the quiet to reminisce about the day before. I wish I could have warned myself not to get attached to this animal. I already felt familiar with her as if she were an old friend from years ago. Now, after reuniting, we were in danger of permanent separation and I couldn't handle it. I looked over at her a few times and she didn't look sad or in pain. She just sat there patiently as if she were also waiting for Marcus to get back. As a person, I feel obligated to fix problems that I come across. However, in situations like that, what could I do? Nothing.

Marcus actually made it back before nightfall. I texted Ann and tried to explain the situation and cancel our debriefing. She texted back with a simple "ok." Marcus seemed very disgruntled and overworked when he came back.

"I'm still working on the blood work for a few of them. They all came back negative except for the Camargue." Rosemary showed immediate defeat once again and found the nearest stool to catch her balance. Marcus also showed his defeat as he said, "I'm so sorry I wish things were better. The good news is that the others do not have the virus, so far. However, the bad news is that the strain found in Belle is aggressive. We're going to do everything we can but it's not looking very good. Needless to say, it's going to be a critical next few hours." Rosemary got up from her stool and began walking outside.

"Sounds like we are going to need some dinner pretty soon." And with that, she was swallowed by the shadowed moonlight.

"Should I go follow her?" I asked Zeke.

"Nah, let her go. If she stays here without anything to do, she'll go crazy. Dinner will at least keep her busy." I took the newly vacant stool and sat down. Marcus spoke.

"When is Mr. Brown supposed to be back?"

"I'm pretty sure he's supposed to be back tomorrow. Isn't that right, Blake?" I shrugged in response to Zeke.

Marcus spoke next. "It might be a matter of keeping her stable enough for Mr. Brown to say goodbye. Didn't Mrs. Brown say this was his favorite?" Zeke nodded, Marcus sighed, and I remained in quiet waiting.

When my grandmother got sick, my family did a lot of quiet waiting. We did a lot of quiet waiting when my grandfather got sick a year later. My mom and I became experts at quiet waiting when we lost my dad. We then perfected our craft in my doctor's office for those few dark months before I met Ann. Now, as I sit in quiet waiting again, it is like greeting an old colleague. However, I haven't always gotten along with this particular colleague. I ignore my frustration and I continue to sit, drooping a little bit. Then, like most of the times I've sat in quiet waiting, I fell asleep.

After

It was hell to sit in the same building as her but be so far away at the same time. I didn't sleep again, and I didn't turn on the TV as my mom suggested, I laid there sorting out the puzzle that was the past few days. It was slowly starting to piece itself together and become less fuzzy. As I pieced together the confusion, I experienced the familiar quiet waiting. I could tell my mom was experiencing it, too. She had resorted to the in-room magazines to occupy her time. She did the same thing at Dr. Sawyer's office years ago. At some point, while I continued to struggle with the concept of the past few days and as I struggled to fight off the quiet waiting, the unofficial paranoid practitioner came back in, still clipboard-less.

Before

I woke up, still slumped on a stool with my eyes still shut. I quietly breathed in through my nose and was greeted by the strong equestrian odor. My fourth sense began to awaken as I heard Marcus and Zeke talking. Marcus was the first I heard.

"…update me as they finish the rest. So far, though, only this one."

Zeke spoke next. "The hard part is figuring out how far along the virus is and how aggressive it is acting towards her."

Then, I heard an unfamiliar voice. It was a male's voice that was low and gentle. "I appreciate all you've done for my sweet Belle here. We don't want you two to overwork and hurt yourselves."

Marcus and Zeke quickly objected. "We'll do everything we can do save her. What's a little sleep compared to a life?"

The man laughed a bit and said, "Well, I can't argue with that." I was all of a sudden too nervous and a little ashamed to open my eyes. I knew who the man was. He was the exact person that I had travelled so far to see. He was the man who held the answer to that stupid question. That question, which seems so trivial now. As I sat there paralyzed, he spoke again. "Is this fella' helping ya'll out?" Marcus and Zeke chuckled a bit.

"Looks like he is helping himself out a bit more right now," Zeke said.

Finally, I spoke. "I'm just resting my eyes." I opened them, and I saw him. The man I looked up to so much, was staring down at me. I slowly stood up and he reached out his hand.

"How do you do, bud? My name's Harriet Brown, been my name ever since I was born." I didn't say anything. I just shook his hand.

Observation: It's easy to critique people who are dumbfounded. I mean, you see this exact situation on TV shows and it's so easy to say something like, "Dude! Just say your name!"

Analysis on Observation: Now, having been the dumbfoundee, it's a lot harder than it seems. My body *actually* forgot how to function.

Conclusion: I have to lay off of people sometimes.

After I did a factory reset on myself, I was able to communicate again.

"My name is Blake and I'm a really big fan, Mr. Brown."

He smiled and said, "Glad to hear it! I also am glad to see you helping Zeke and Marcus here. These are great kids and they'll do right by you."

"Kids?" said Zeke as Marcus elbowed him.

"Son, when you're as old as me, everyone is a kid. Now, why don't we see if Rosie is done with dinner." He left the stables and headed towards the house.

"I couldn't have been asleep long I guess," I spoke towards Zeke and Marcus.

"No, not at all. Maybe twenty minutes or so? Rosemary went up to the house about 45 minutes ago. Mr. Brown must really love this horse, because he rushed back as soon as Rosemary told him about her condition."

"How is she?" I inquired.

"Well," Marcus spoke relatively confidently. "I checked some vitals right before Mr. Brown came back. I'll check them again shortly. Why don't you go up and grab some food? I'll be there directly." Zeke and I nodded and headed up towards the house.

"Anytime Marcus and I must stay late with any of the animals, the Brown's always invite us to their table for dinner. I guess it's this unspoken agreement between us." Zeke told me as we walked through the dark field listening to the crickets' symphony.

When Zeke and I made it to the kitchen, Mr. Brown was laying out the dishes on the table that had expanded to accommodate the extra guests. "Sit wherever you'd like to. We try not to have assigned seats at the table. It's important to shake things up when you get as old as us," he said as he laid the last few utensils down.

"You just try to keep me on my toes, love." Rosemary said, flinging water at him while she washed her hands.

"It smells really delicious!"

"Well, thank you, Zeke! I made it myself." When Mr. Brown said this, Rosemary turned around and shot him a look I had yet to see her give anyone. Mr. Brown leaped out of his chair, put his hands up in surrender and started to laugh. Immediately, the fictional anger and tension in the kitchen evaporated and was replaced with Mr. Brown's goofy giddiness.

"Why don't you boys go and wash up in the bathroom." Both Zeke and I nodded as to acknowledge Rosemary's request and made our way into the bathroom.

"How is he acting like this when the situation is this morbid?" I asked Zeke while waiting for my turn at the sink.

"He always has an optimistic attitude until its outcome is revealed. Trust me, if things go south, he'll behave differently. Personally though, I appreciate his current attitude."

When we were ready to sit down and eat, Marcus knocked on the back door, entered, washed his hands, and sat down in the last unoccupied sat. Everyone understood that the dinner table was meant for "pleasant conversation only." Mr. Brown was the first to initiate conversation by asking me to pray.

"You are a praying man?" he said with the inflection of a question.

"Yes sir, but probably not as much as I should." So, I prayed. Now, I don't know if there is a Likert measurement for prayers, but if there was, everyone at the table would be bubbling in: 'Ineffective, would not ask to pray again.' "Dear God, (ah yes, I am writing a letter to God) thank you so much for everything you've given us (well, I guess that about sums it all up). I'm thankful to be surrounded by wonderful people (that is true). I'm thankful to have a roof over my head and food in my stomach (pretty good food, at that). Please help us figure out what is wrong with Belle. Help Marcus to do the things he needs to do in order to get the attention she needs."

"However, let Your will be done. We understand that You work in ways that we are unable to understand." Mr. Brown added

his addendum and then smiled, winked, and nodded at me to
continue.

"…uh, yeah. Also, uh…lead our conversation and our week,
that they may be pleasing to You. Finally, please watch over Ann
and get her the attention that she needs. Amen?"

I finished it up with a question, but everyone took it as an
absolute and replied together, "Amen."

We began to make our plates and the room was filled with
the clinging of silverware and plates. Again, though Mr. Brown
directed the initial conversation at me.

"Whereabouts are you from, Blake?" Even though it's easy
to assume that Rosemary told him my name, there is something
magical about your idol calling you by name.

"I'm from a small town called Middleton. It's some far ways
west of here."

Brown smiled with his mouth full of jambalaya. "How'd you
wind up all the way over here?"

"Mostly the stress of everything going on at home. There was
an incident that occurred, not too far from my home. That, with the
stress of picking a school to study at, forced me to leave for a bit. To
get a breath of fresh air, so to speak." I took a bite of the Cajun dish.
It was delicious.

"Did you come here all by your lonesome?" Mr. Brown
continued.

I shook my head. "No, sir." The thought of Ann flashed in
my mind, but I decided not to expand upon my response. As a

gentleman and a knower of the small things in life, Mr. Brown did not pry.

"Rosie here tells me you've been working here for a few days." I nodded but did not respond due to the shrimp, chicken, and Cajun rice in my mouth. Again, Mr. Brown understood, but that didn't stop him from asking questions. "So, do you have an interest in animals?" This time I waited to take my next bite, so I could respond.

"Yes, I think so." Everyone at the table sort of chortled. Before Mr. Brown spoke again, Rosemary did.

"That's how I am, Blake. However, I can only talk with the animals so much before Harry and Zeke start to look at me like I'm crazy or something."

"You are crazy," Zeke and Mr. Brown said simultaneously through smiling mouths full of food.

"I still like to talk to other folk though. That's why I pick up a shift a few times a week at the convenience store down a ways. This allows me to fulfill my lifelong dream of selling marshmallows and apples to younger kids on an existential adventure." I laughed a little bit.

It was quiet for a few moments while we continued to eat. Marcus and Zeke talked a little about how things were going and answered a few questions from Mr. Brown as well. Marcus talked about Tasha and Zeke talked about his past semester. It seems that they had their lives together more than I did.

At the next lull in conversation, Mr. Brown turned his attention back towards me. "So, what are you interested in, son?" My heart started to pound a little bit. This was my opportunity to ask my incredibly inconsequential inquiry.

"I'm actually quite fascinated by well-known quotes and their situational context as well as their origin." I said while keeping my cool as well as an ice cube under the blistering sun.

"That's a unique interest. Is there a particular quote that you are most fond of?" Before I could speak and as if it were a literary device to demonstrate my spout of poor coincidences, the rain came down.

Now, growing up in the bipolar climate of Tennessee, I, as well as everyone at this table had experienced a sudden unexplainable and sometimes metaphorical thunderstorm. From raining out our sporting events to raining on our parade, we have seen it all. However, this one felt off and we knew something more was going on. As Marcus, Zeke, Mr. Brown, Rosemary, and I all immediately rushed outside towards the stables, it was obvious we were all on the same page. We sloshed through the grass and made it to the stables soaking wet. The rain pounded against the tin roof above our heads and the thunder roared in the nearby distance. One of the animal hands, whose name I did not know, assured Mr. Brown that the other animals were being placed into shelter as soon as possible. This gave us the ability to focus solely on the horses and Belle.

"We have to make sure that Belle and the others are staying as dry as they can. Try to keep the rain water out of their drinking water as well, none of them need the extra bacteria in their systems, especially Belle." Marcus shouted these instructions over the piercing pings of rain overhead. This was a relatively easy task to undertake considering we were in the stables and the biggest protection form the rain was the loud roof and the large door. After securing the door and knowing I could do nothing for the integrity of the roof, I awaited further instruction. This thunderstorm was not out of the ordinary. It was no different than any other rainstorm any of us had come in contact with before. However, like I had stated, this one came with an emotional weight we had not yet understood. Similar to the way ominous music crescendos to foreshadow an intense moment in a movie or show, so the rain continued to pour as it foreshadowed the darkening events that laid before us.

After

I looked out of my hospital window as the rain continued to poor on the innocent victims only a few floors below.

Nine

Before

Marcus, Zeke, and I continued to sit with Belle as the night dragged on and the rain refused to cease. By around 11:00 P.M., the rain had slowed to a less threatening hum. Mr. Brown and Rosemary had been in and out of the stables as they had to check on the other animals. They made sure to stop in the house and change into warmer clothes and to grab umbrellas. I found myself worrying about them and their age, as they made their rounds to check on the other livestock.

"The last thing we need is for the Browns to end up sick because of all of this rain," Marcus said aloud what I had been thinking. I looked over at Belle who was still as calm as could be.

"She doesn't have much left in her, does she?" I asked Marcus. Though calm, I could sense the fatigue radiating off of her.

Marcus nodded solemnly and said, "It's not much longer now." The way Marcus said this struck me as comforting. Instead of talking about death as an absolute he spoke of it like the last leg of a journey. It seemed accurate to me. Belle is almost finished with her journey which is not a sad thing, but bittersweet.

"Is WEE is something that can really take a horse out this fast?" I asked Marcus, still not wanting to believe it to be true. He again nodded solemnly.

"It's rare, but it happens. In this situation, however, it's not so much that the virus has worked fast, it's that we don't know how long the virus has been plotting its attack." *I guess that's true,* I thought.

The large door to the stable opened which announced Mr. Brown's arrival for the last time. "All of the other animals are put away and out of this horrible storm." Despite the dreary weather outside and the monotonous atmosphere in here, Mr. Brown still had life and joy in his cheeks. "How's my girl doing?" he said, as he made his way over to the three of us gathered around her stall.

"It's not looking good, sir." Marcus said, speaking for the group. Immediately, I saw Mr. Brown's giddiness dissipate and like Zeke said, he began to behave differently.

"Okay, we need to start talking about some of our options." He and Marcus moved over to the other side of the barn and began to talk in whispers, so Zeke and I could not hear. Zeke looked mournful over at Belle and then over at me. I didn't have to be a farm hand or an expert in such a field to understand what conversation was being had. It's not fair for any animal to suffer in the way that Belle is suffering right now with the inability to fight.

When I was about five years old, my family had this beautiful golden lab. Being five years old and full of excitement, the dog and I quickly became best friends. With no brother or sister to force my energy upon, my only outlet was Bo. With no other dog or animal companion to force his energy upon, Bo's only outlet was myself. Until a week before my 10th birthday, Bo and I played as faithful friends. Until a week before my 10th birthday, Bo and I would take a walk every day up and down the street. Until a week before my 10th birthday, I left an extra blanket at the end of my bed for Bo to sleep on. Until a week before my 10th birthday, the only thing I wanted was a camera to take pictures with Bo. On my 10th birthday, the only thing I wanted was to have my best friend back. It was my parents who made the decision to bring him in and put him to sleep instead of letting him live out a painful and cancer filled existence. I, being only 9 years, 11 months, and 23 days old, had no say in what would happen to my best friend of almost 5 years. Half of my life was spent with him. After he left, instead of spending my days playing with Bo, I spent my days talking to a doctor. A doctor who asked me about Bo. A doctor who asked why I still go on walks every day up and down the street even though Bo is gone. A doctor who asked why I still leave an extra blanket out at the end of my bed before I go to sleep. I talked with this doctor for months before I started to talk to the girl who moved in down the street from me. Then, my parents didn't seem to think it necessary for me to talk to the doctor anymore.

In the case of Bo, my parents had the same talk with the veterinarian as Mr. Brown was having with Marcus.

"He hates having these conversations," Zeke said, as he saved me from my own thoughts. "He always feels like he played a big part in how it ends, no matter what they end up choosing. You can't win in that situation." I nodded as Zeke spoke. I wasn't sure what I could do to stop any of this from happening.

I watched helplessly as Mr. Brown hung his head and Marcus closed his eyes and pressed his lips together. They both walked back over after a few moments of silent prayer. Mr. Brown grabbed one of the vacant stools and sat with us. I knelt next to Belle and pet her mane. She looked at me with obligement. Marcus continued to repeat, "Not much longer now, baby," as I slowly moved up and down her mane. We sat out there with her for a few more hours, and when the rain finally ceased, it happened. It happened no different than if she were to fall asleep.

Marcus, his team, and Zeke stayed a little longer to handle the remains. Mr. Brown and I made our way back up to the house as the morning sun began to rise. The birds serenaded us as we walked, and other than the loss of a friend, and the wet ground, no evidence remained of the darkened night that we all witnessed. Rosemary and Mr. Brown embraced as we entered the kitchen. Unable to look at the scene, I made my way upstairs to where my belongings were placed. I took off my shoes, got undressed, and laid down on the bed. I fell asleep before I could pull the covers over my body.

I had definitely not gotten up early enough for Rosemary and not early enough to do any of my chores that I needed to do. However, I knew I would not be penalized for this. When I showered, dressed, and made it down stairs, Mr. Brown and Rosemary were sitting in the kitchen.

"You know, I think they invented living rooms for casual occupancy," I told them as I sat with them at the table. It was feeble attempt for a joke and they replied with a feeble attempt to acknowledge it.

"I believe the living room was *designed* not invented," Mr. Brown replied looking up from a newspaper.

"I'm sorry I slept in so much," I told them.

"After the night we had, son, I don't blame you or hold it against you." Mr. Brown took a sip from a mug which looked like coffee but smelled like tea. He saw me eyeing it funny. "It's supposed to be good for my blood sugar." He took another sip.

"What would you like me to accomplish today?" I asked Rosemary trying to sound eager, but the hints of fatigue and sadness seeped through the barriers.

"I think you can just help me in the garden, if that's okay? It's already fairly late in the afternoon so we don't have a lot of time before the sun goes down." I nodded, thankful for the peace that comes with working in the garden. Rosemary put down her own mug, kissed Mr. Brown on the cheek, and made her way out the door and into the nearby garden. I closed the gate behind me as I found myself amongst the humble germination.

"I have something I want to show you first." Rosemary said gently. I grinned a little bit, knowing what she may want to show me. I had not forgotten my few hours in the garden on my first day. "I want to show you hope."

She knelt beside the area where I had planted a few tomato seeds and pointed out the smallest stem coming just a few centimeters out of the ground. "Tomato seeds don't usually germinate until about the fifth or sixth day after planting, but one of your little guys is jumpin' at the seams to grow up." I knelt beside her and leaned in very close to examine my handiwork. I was speechless. I had grown plants in science classes before for a grade, but never had I put so much care into planting something with the objective to see it thrive for others.

"Life will sometimes hand you a magical moment. Savor it." I quoted with my eyes starting to precipitate.

"It's been a few days since you quoted anything there, darling." Rosemary observed as I spoke her husband's words.

"It's because I've been exposed to some of the greatest quotes by you, your husband, Zeke, and Marcus. I felt no reason to bring in any outsiders to ruin the intimacy."

"You have had your fair share of quotes these past few days too, love. Don't think they've gone unnoticed." I blushed, and Rosemary and I got to work. We worked for only a few hours before it began to get dark. We planted a few new seeds and stuck forks around the new sprouts to, "ward off any hungry critters."

We made our way inside where, this time, Mr. Brown was fixing dinner over the stove.

"What are you making, love?" Rosemary asked as she started to wash her hands in the sink.

"Well, seeing as we all slept through the most important part of the day, I made some breakfast for dinner." He kissed his wife and continued to flip the bacon that was sizzling in his pan. I walked to the bathroom to clean my hands.

"Why don't you go upstairs and make sure you are all packed up and ready to leave in the morning. I'm sure you don't want us giving you more work in the morning," Mr. Brown said as I came back into the kitchen.

"I would actually love to spend much more time here with you lovely folk, but I should start my leg of the journey back home," I spoke softly.

"We understand, son," Mr. Brown said.

I nodded, ran upstairs, and started to pack my stuff. I noticed that all my clothes had been washed while I was sleeping the day away. I assumed it was Rosemary and I was very grateful. She had also put my cell-phone on the bedside table. I had completely forgotten about that old thing. I unlocked it and found only one text message. It was from my mom. *I love you honey, I know you are safe and I'm excited to see you home soon. Things are beginning to return to normalcy here. Text me, when you are on your way back.*

Even hundreds of miles away, I could feel the comforting parental embrace of my mom. I texted her back and told her that I was okay and would be heading back the next day. I then, decided to finally text Ann.

Me (5:45 P.M.): *Hey, sorry I haven't been able to talk much the past few das. A lot has been going on.*

Me (5:45 P.M.): *days**

Her (5:47 P.M.): *Don't worry about it. I knew what I was signing up for ;)*

Me (5:48 P.M.): *Well, if you want, I can head out tonight. I can rent one more hotel room and I can tell you all about it.*

Her (5:50 P.M.): *If any other guy texted me this, I'd tell them to get lost. But, I know you have no secret motives. Sounds like a plan. ETA?*

Me (5:52 P.M.): *How about I text you after I finish eating and I'll meet you at the same hotel from a few nights ago. You need a ride?*

Her (5:52 P.M.): *What if you just meet me at the hotel from a few nights ago?*

Her (5:53 P.M.): *JINKS! No, I don't need a ride. I'll see you there in a bit!*

Me (5:54 P.M.): *Yes ma'am.*

I quickly finished my packing and tied up my fancy Wal-Mart bag luggage. I ran outside to put my bag in the car and then went back into the kitchen. Dinner was pretty much ready. We all sat down to eat, at different seats than the night before.

This time, Mr. Brown prayed. "Well, hello, Lord, I just want to thank You for the past day. Thank You for the beautiful life of Belle and the time that we were able to spend with her. It's no surprise to us that we are saddened by her loss and we pray that You fill us with Your peace. Please also be with Marcus and Zeke and help them to realize that it was neither of their faults and that You have a bigger and better plan, and that they should not blame themselves. Thank You also for our new-found friend, Blake. Please be with him on his journey home. As always, thank You for our health and happiness. Finally, as Blake requested yesterday please watch over Ann. We pray all of this in Your name, Lord. Amen." Rosemary and I responded alike. Mr. Brown's prayer was so elegant and sweet, and I was jealous of the way he could craft words into beautiful quotes as well as beautiful prayers. He also seemed to have been listening to my prayer from the previous day as he added in Ann's name. My inspiration and awe of Mr. Brown continued to grow.

We began eating and for the last time, Mr. Brown directed initial conversation at me. "So, Blake, I don't think you ever ended up telling me what your favorite quote was." As he said this, he winked over at Rosemary and I could tell that she put him up to this. I was embarrassed because of how trivial I still thought the question to be as well as nervous because I didn't want to sound like a blabbering idiot.

"Oh, right. Uh…" My fear was already starting to become a reality. Eventually I found my verbal footing and took my step.

"Twenty years from now, you'll be more disappointed by the things you didn't do than by the one's you did do. So, throw off the bowlines, sail away from the safe harbor. Explore. Dream. Discover." While I spoke the familiar quote, Mr. Brown smiled.

"Catch the trade-winds in your sails," he added as we all sat for a few moments. "This quote is one of my favorites as well. Where did you hear it?"

I responded fairly quickly with, "It was over the chalkboard in my homeroom a few years ago."

He continued to smile. "Sounds like your teacher had excellent taste in quotes."

This time, I smiled. "She did. She definitely did. However, my problem with this quote is the origin." I waited in case he had anything to add. He didn't. "A few of my teachers believe this quote to come from Mark Twain, but I don't think that's right." I waited again.

"Who do you think this quote is from?"

I looked at him. "I think it came from you." There were a few moments of silence as he pondered this.

"I am honored you would think such a thing. However, I am sorry to inform you that mine was not the tongue at the origin of this quote." I was completely crushed. I was shattered into many pieces and believed myself to be unable to piece back together. I couldn't believe it. I couldn't believe I had completely wasted my time and the Brown's time with my whimsical fantasies. How dare me to have intruded on these pure lives for my own selfish agenda. I wanted to get up and leave. I wanted to get up and drive back home as fast as I could, but this would be rude, and I cannot impose my selfishness or discourtesy on this beautiful couple any longer.

Mr. Brown spoke again seeing how much I was crushed by his response. "I am very certain that Mr. Twain was not at the base of this quote either, son." I nodded, feeling a small glimmer of hope and realizing the world as I know will remain intact, however embarrassed I may be.

"I still think you have amazing literary work, Mr. Brown," I said, trying to make up for the last few moments.

"Well, I appreciate it, son. I am glad that others found my words meaningful and have taken to heart what my meager self thinks of this beautiful world." Rosemary smiled at her husband's response.

"I'm glad I get to share this beautiful world with you." They smiled at each other and then Mr. Brown grabbed Rosemary's old hand and kissed it ever so gently. I can only imagine how many gentle pecks that hand has received as her and Mr. Brown have grown old together. I can't wait to have something like that in my life. I want to be able to have that when I am an old man looking back on the world that I was so lucky enough to live in.

I spoke my thoughts out loud, saying, "I hope that one day I can find someone to share the world with. It is wide, and it will take two to see everything, I think."

Mr. Brown raised his glass and said, "Well said, son." I decided now would be an appropriate time to ask if I could shorten my stay by leaving tonight instead of in the morning as was their impression.

"I hate to ask this because I am very fond of our arrangement here. I've enjoyed working with you the past few days and I've enjoyed getting to know you two as a couple and individuals. However, do you mind if I leave after dinner instead of in the morning? I promise it is nothing against you. I have kept my friend in the dark for too long and it isn't fair for me to do it anymore. If anything, you've both taught me the importance of putting others first as well as taking care of yourself and I am very, very grateful for this lesson. You've both given me confidence, friendship, love, and above all hope. Hope for myself, hope for the future, and hope for the beauty of this world." I stopped and let my words hang in the air allowing Rosemary and Mr. Brown to take them as needed.

"We are very gracious for your company, dear. We are more than happy to oblige your request to leave a night early. Thank you so much for your help here the past few days and we are so sorry about what happened to Belle. She was a precious, gentle, and loving creature and it's a shame it had to come while you were working and as soon as you began to take a liking to her." Rosemary smiled at me and then looked at Mr. Brown to finish her thought for her.

"Son, life is unfair that way. Now, I'm going to give you some advice you may have heard before. That advice is: don't ever forget that it takes only one person or even one idea to completely change your life forever."

My heart was full as I finished eating my breakfast for dinner. I was able to hear all about Rosemary and Mr. Brown's first date and how they met. I was also granted the opportunity to hear about their kids and where they are now. It was a beautiful way to end a beautiful few days filled with life, death, happiness, and despair. Above all of it though, it was filled with faith, hope, and love. As the apostle Paul wrote in his letter to the Corinthians, "And now these three remain: faith, hope, and love. But the greatest of these is love."

I texted Ann as I got in my car and pulled out of the long driveway that led up to the quaint farm house. She responded saying she was on her way to the hotel as well. I put the envelope of cash that Rosemary gave me as I headed out in my glove compartment, so I wouldn't spend it all before I even got the hotel

Ten

Before

I arrived at the hotel before Ann did. So, I paid for the room, and then carried up my small bag of freshly cleaned clothes. Before long, there was a knock on the door and Ann entered, beautiful as ever.

"Well, hello! Long time, no see," she said as she put her stuff on the bed. "I am so tired. I'm so ready to go to bed, but not until I hear every detail about your past few days." So, without wasting a beat, I started to tell her everything that had happened since our first and only evening debriefing. She was as attentive to my story in the hotel room as she was in the creamery a few days prior. She laughed and smiled at the parts she was supposed to laugh and smile on. She was incredibly saddened at the parts that she was supposed to be incredibly saddened by and she felt victorious on the parts she was supposed to feel victorious on. And, during all the parts of the story, good or bad, she looked stunning.

"So, now was the moment you and I had been waiting for. He finally gave me an opportunity to ask the question and I choked. I freaked out!" I was saying. Ann gasped: an expert on her lines in the script. "Eventually, something came over me and I asked it. I said everything that I had wanted to say to him. I told him the quote and I told him I thought he was the one that said it." I stopped for a beat.

"And...?" Ann pressed.

My shoulders sank, and I said, "He said it wasn't him." Ann looked astonished.

"So, it was Twain?"

"Well, he said he was fairly certain it was not Twain, either." I was sort of annoyed with the answer we received.

Ann spoke. "Well, this type of stuff happens in life. You start a journey thinking it will get you to one place and you find yourself at a completely different place than you expected."

I nodded. "Yeah, that's what I thought." I then asked if she wanted to tell me about her few days with her aunt. However, she did not seem excited about the suggestion.

"I'd much rather just go to bed. Is that okay?" Part of me appreciated her decline as my fatigue began to catch back up with me yet again. We both laid down on the bed facing each other. We observed each other's faces while we slowly started to fall asleep. I tried to capture every curve and shape in her face but was unable to do it in the time my body gave me before it started to relax. She reached out and grabbed my hand as we lay there. Still looking at each other, still studying, and our fingers intertwined. I closed my eyes, finally giving in to the physical pressures to fall asleep. Just before I finally did, I felt Ann's hand yank away from me.

I woke up early that morning back in my bedroom. It felt like a normal morning. It felt like everything was running the way that the universe had planned it to run: smoothly. I looked at my clock: 2:37 A.M. What had woken me up? I didn't know. I laid there quietly, listening to the sound of my heart beating quietly against my chest. The interesting things about the skin, is that it covers up chaos, similar to the architecture of a house. Behind the skin of your body, you have roughly thirty-seven trillion individual cells working non-stop, so you can be you. Though organization might exist, it is still a lot of energy and power that most people don't realize. Most people take that for granted. The architecture of a house, is similarly designed to hide chaos like the skin of your body. Just looking at a house will not tell you anything about the type of lives that exist within the walls. I want to believe God did this on purpose when designing the human body. We are allowed to hide our flaws and chaos within ourselves. For example, there is no shame in working tirelessly (like our bodies do), but there *is* shame in seeking attention for your tiredness. Are you working for the people around you, or are you working for yourself? That is why the skin exists, there is no reason to flaunt your hard work. You may be proud of it, but one shouldn't seek to brag about how hard they work. Each of us have trillions of cells that keep our body running and each of us have problems that we must deal with. There should be no competition of stress or any intention of apathy for someone equally stressed or hard working.

The world is a body, and all of us (as humans) are individual cells, working tirelessly to make our world continually exist. The world takes us for granted, and sometimes does not treat us the best, but we trudge on, understanding the greater good. Our galaxy is a body, and all of the worlds and enormously massed bodies in space are individual cells, working tirelessly to make our galaxy continually exist. The universe is a body, and all of the galaxies are individual cells, working tirelessly to make our universe continually exist. What is the universe then? Who does the Universe work for? Is it us? Is the entire fundamental fabric of existence just a complex paradox that starts and ends with us? If so, where is the line drawn?

William Shakespeare is credited with the quote: "'Tis in ourselves that we are thus or thus. Our bodies are our gardens, to the which our wills are gardeners." I believe Shakespeare is telling the audience that what we are is up to us and how we use our bodies. How we use those trillions of cells, is who we will become and eventually how people will see us. It's important to master their technique and use them correctly.

I realize that this is not the typical thoughts of a teenager on a rainy summer break. But I needed to plan. I needed to understand the significance of my actions before I performed said action. When I was younger, my mom always said, "Think about what you say before you say it, Blake!" Why is this rule only applied to speech? As I continued to lay there, my phone rang. It was him.

Me: Hello?

Him: Hey there, champ! How's it going?

Me: Uhm, good? It's really early here, Dad. Are you alright?

Him: Oh shoot! I'm sorry. I miscalculated the time change. I just wanted to let you know that I am on my way home. My flight leaves really soon, so I should be landing in Nashville by the time you get off work.

Me: Awesome!

Him: Are you still wanting to come and pick me up?

Me: Yes, of course! It'll be a nice road trip. I need to get out of town for a bit, even if it is only a few hours.

Him: Great! Well, they're calling for my flight, so I'll let you go. Don't get too lonely on the road trip. Play some N'sync or something. Love you, buddy.

Me: Love you, too!

I mustered enough strength to roll out of bed. I looked like pure and unadulterated beauty. My hair allowed for a nesting space to nearby birds. My breath was a great defense mechanism to anyone within twenty feet of me. I was ready to take on the world...right after a shower.

The shower is a wonderful place to think. There is nothing to do in there *but* think (I guess one should attempt to cleanse themselves). Whilst cleansing, my mind wandered to school (of all things). Starting my senior year began stressing me out a couple of days ago. During my other three years of high school, I was so concerned about keeping my friends and passing classes, that I didn't get a chance to stop and enjoy high school. Growing up to the mature age I am now, everyone has told me that senior year is made for enjoyment. I hope that is the case. I need a little bit of a break from the chaos and torment that is high school.

I turned off the water and grabbed a towel to retain my modesty whilst searching for physical fabric to cover myself with. I proceeded from there, as I have done every morning that summer. Get dressed: Check. Pick up room: Check. Eat Breakfast: Check. Turn on the news: Check.

The news is the exact same thing every day, which is probably why my mom and dad never watch it. They hear the news about a week late from everybody else. Which isn't really that big of a deal because it always sounds like: "Someone was hurt today at the hands of another person," "A sports team had a great upset today," "A celebrity flaunts their famous status by disobeying the natural laws of everyone else." Today was no different but there was nothing noteworthy or unusual. I grabbed my stuff and headed to work.

Of all the places that I could have worked, I chose to work behind a desk. I worked at the Middleton driver's license bureau. It obviously was not a prestigious job, but it gave me something to do on the weekends and after school. For the most part, I sat around in a tin building making copies of automobile information and filing the aforementioned information. It's not a horrible job, it's just boring.

I wouldn't call myself a boring person. I would love to go on crazy fun adventures, but it's just not plausible for someone about to enter their senior year of high school. I am forced to rely on my acumen to keep me out of trouble because there is too much to be done this year. There is too much to worry about. I have to make sure I don't ruin everything I've worked for. I have to find a college to go to. I have to go to that college at a reasonable price that is affordable for me and my parents. The scary part of that isn't about the money, it's about leaving. Leaving will be the hardest thing that I could ever do. It's a scary thought to know that the last eighteen years of your life would soon be just a memory. To start anew is terrifying. When a neighborhood undergoes gentrification, everything is torn down and rebuilt. Essentially, that is what I am doing with my life, and I've never been so scared. Now, I know that "an ending is just a new beginning" or whatever, but that doesn't mean you don't have fear when an ending comes.

In the case of beginnings and endings I prefer to follow the founder of Taoism, Lao Tzu's philosophy. He said, "New beginnings are often disguised as painful endings." I'm not a pessimistic person (nor am I a Taoist), but I'm also not an unrealistic person. I know what is attainable and what is not which may actually fall under a few Taoist beliefs.

The town was acting normally today, and I enjoyed waving to the friendly faces as I grabbed some snacks for the road and found

my car. I pulled out onto Navy Rd. and passed the library and the
post office. I remembered going to the library with my dad every
Friday after he got off work. I always went straight for the kid's
section and would pick out something like Clifford or a Scooby Doo
action book. I know I don't seem like the type of kid who would
read *Clifford the Big Red Dog*, but there was something about having
a giant red dog that seemed cool to me. Apparently, I liked cool dogs
because Clifford was rideable and Scooby solved mysteries. It
doesn't get more kick-ass than that. It also doesn't get much simpler
than that. Little kids are so innocent, and they don't have to worry
about anything. They just have fun and enjoy themselves. Why can't
that always be the case with humans? Why are the children learning
from the adults? The adults should actually be learning from the
children. They definitely seem to enjoy themselves much more.

The first thirty minutes of the drive was as normal as I had
expected it to be. The normalcy was just a vast highway. I'm not
talking about a metaphorical highway that symbolized the "stop and
go traffic" that was my life. I'm not talking about metaphorical brake
lights. I'm not talking about metaphorical flat tires that symbolize
my failures. I am talking about a literal highway, with literal brake
lights, and (knock on wood) no flat tires. Luckily for me, the drive
didn't feel as long as it was and within a few hours I had reached the
airport. My dad, with perfect timing, was waiting for me at the front
doors with his luggage in hand. "Hey! You made it! Good to see
you, buddy!" He got in the car, closed the door, and began

immediately spouting off about his deployment. As I pulled back onto the highway to head back to Middleton, I woke up.

I was feeling slightly panicked and felt myself slipping. I opened my eyes and saw Ann lying next to me. A calming wave washed over me which kept me rooted in reality. *You're fine. Everything is okay.* I told myself. Things haven't felt this bad since my 10th birthday. I laid there, breathing quietly. I must have woken up Ann because she rolled over to look at me.

"Hey, are you alright?" she asked groggily.

"Yeah, I'm sorry if I woke you up." Instead of rolling back over, she inched towards me and slung her arm over my chest.

"I've had fun with you on our adventure, Mr. Harper." A solemn tone seeped through her words and tickled my neck. She continued, "I'm sorry it has to come to an end." I grabbed her hand which was soft and gentle to the touch.

"All things must come to an end, even good things," I said, roughly quoting Geoffrey Chaucer.

"One of the great tragedies of this world," Ann replied sadly. We laid there, procrastinating our inevitable journey back to reality and away from our fleeting fantasies. I continued to hold onto her hand and could feel the strong tension growing between us. I didn't want anything to happen, however. It would add an extra element to our chemical reaction that would grant immediate pleasure and satisfaction but would eventually ruin everything. I understood this as I laid there next to her soft body and maintained my self-control. My admiration for her wasn't a sexual desire, but instead was emotional awe. Even if I did want something physical to happen, part of me knew it was impossible. Eventually, we knew there was no more delaying the inevitable. Without much conversation and after our anticlimactic night, we cleaned up, showered, and checked out.

The Intrepid needed gas once more so we pulled into the gas station just before the ramp onto I-40 W. I used some of the money I received from Rosemary to fill up the tank. After her generous payment, I would still have enough to pay off my credit payments from the nights in the different hotels and our infrequent trips for food and supplies. I finished gassing up, got back in the car and headed towards I-40 W, partly wanting the trip to never end and partly wanting to be back in the comfortable town that I knew and loved.

We drove for a few miles down the road before I decided to tell Ann about my dream the previous night. I told her all about taking the trip to Nashville by myself. I told her about how lonely it was and less exciting than my trip with her.

"This isn't a trip that I would want to take with anyone else."

She smiled at me. "Why did you go on the trip by yourself?"

"That's the weird thing. I was picking my dad up from the airport. It was the same flight and gate from 13 years ago." She thought about it for a few moments before she spoke again.

"How have you felt since?"

"I've been okay. I was wavering this morning, but I think I'm okay now."

"Do you miss him?" She asked.

"Always," I responded.

We didn't speak much after that, so I turned on the radio to drown out the silence. When the volume was turned up, she reached out for my empty right hand and held on tight. I continued to drive as her grip loosened while she gave in to the highway's hypnotic hum. After a cycle of about 25 well known songs and about 15 unknown, I looked over at Ann and wondered how much longer until we would arrive in our familiar town. She was asleep, so I snuck my phone out of my pocket and began typing in the address. I periodically looked up at the road to make sure I wasn't veering and then glanced back down at my phone. I was typing in the address when the car shook. I dropped my phone and glanced up. I had started to drive off onto the shoulder. I jerked the steering wheel to the left to get back onto the road. Ann woke up and screamed. I made it back onto the road but had lost control of the car. I kept my hands on the steering wheel as I watched the road spin in circles ahead of me. I saw Ann's hand on my knee but no longer felt it. I looked up at her and she seemed calm and somber as she attempted to smile at me. My heart dropped when I saw her head jerk and the darkness swallowed us.

Eleven

During

I woke up in a hospital bed back in Middleton. It was raining outside. I wasn't quite sure how I had gotten there because all I remembered was the crash. I felt my body lunge forward and reaching out for Ann before everything went black. I reached out again, and I felt a hand. It was my mother's, of course. She never ceased to amaze me with her punctuality. "Mom, where's Ann? Is she okay? Did she get hurt?" I started to sit myself up, but I couldn't find the strength. I was too sore from what I assumed could only be a broken rib or two. My mom helped lay me back down as she began to quiet me. "Shhh, honey, it's okay. Just lay back." As my head hit the pillow, I descended back into the looming hands of sleep.

I woke again a few hours later. The sky was now wet, dark, and faded, as what little moonlight there was, shone through the blinds. This time, I allowed myself a few moments to seep back into full consciousness. My mother was now gone, and I felt a surge of guilty love creep up my body. At that moment, I experienced a deep pain and sickness for myself. How could I have been so selfish to leave her like that with no warning? She could have needed me while I was gone, and I couldn't be there for her. Now, when I needed her, she was gone. Earlier I appreciated her punctuality, but now I cursed it because I know she is somewhere else because the doctors would not let her spend the night. I was quickly reminded of the first time I spent the night in the hospital by myself.

I was five years old and was asked to come into the hospital by the doctor I had been seeing. According to the doctor, I was showing signs of severe distress due to the absence of my dad. I had been having vivid dreams and hallucinations which consisted of my dad playing with me the same way he did when he was on leave. I refused to believe that he was gone and wasn't coming back. Before making any psychological diagnoses, she wanted to observe me throughout the night and refused to let my mom stay with me to avoid faulty data collection. My mom begged the doctors to let her stay with me, but they wouldn't allow it, and there was nothing she could do. She understood as a patient but disagreed as a mother. I remembered for the first time waking up and her not being at my side and feeling so terrified. I was too young to understand "flying away from the nest," but old enough to understand that, like my dad, she couldn't always be there for me. It was then, that I realized I needed to start fixing some problems for myself to my maximum capabilities.

As I laid in a hospital bed again, having aged a long thirteen years, I had grasped both concepts. While it is an extremely cliché metaphor: I was on the edge of the nest, expanding my wings, about to jump. I knew that when I fell I must figure out how to soar back into the air. It was my mother's job to watch me and hope that I make the right decisions. I felt as though my trip to Nashville was not the right decision.

I pushed the call button on my remote control and waited for a nurse to come in. A slender middle-aged man came into the room with his doctor's coat on. His hair was a little frazzled and he lacked the official "I am a doctor" clipboard. He seemed paranoid as he closed the door behind him. "Mr. Harper?" he croaked.

"Yeah?" I responded shortly.

"How are you feeling?" he asked gently.

"I'm feeling sore, but I guess that's what is expected after a car accident, right?" It was a poor attempt at a joke.

"Yes, I guess so," he replied with a forced chuckle. "Surprisingly, your physical health is not our number one concern. You were very lucky in this car accident, suffering only minor bruises."

"How is Ann?" I asked, not really wanting to hear the answer.

I'm not an expert deduction artist, but I was able deduce the uncomplicated puzzle that the clipboard-less man introduced.

Observation: He seemed a little confused at my mention of Ann

Analysis on Observation: This could mean he has no idea who I am talking about or maybe he just doesn't have her as a patient.

Conclusion: Well…I don't really have one, I am thoroughly confused.

He looked at me with intense concern. "Yes, Mr. Harper, you mentioned Ann numerous times in your unconscious state." I must have looked embarrassed because he quickly added, "You didn't say anything incriminating, of course. I can only assume you were talking about Ann Paige, yes?" I nodded my head with that same confusion. He lowered his head, solemnly. He didn't have to say anything to communicate his message with me. My head began to spin and then the room began to spin. I couldn't focus on the words that this man was speaking to me. Ann Paige was not gone. I refused to believe it. The man, knowing that I was in complete disarray quietly left me to my thoughts. He closed the door and I felt the solitude envelope me and soon I feel back towards the blackening pit of unconsciousness.

It was still raining when I woke up for the third time. My mother was back and the man lacking the official clipboard was not. I was incredibly confused and disoriented still but I needed answers and I needed them from my mother. She saw me wake up and she was at my side immediately.

"I need to know what is going on, Mom," I told her gently as she grabbed my hand. She nodded slowly and sat back down in her chair not letting go of my hand and started to explain everything.

"It happened in the early morning the day that you left. According to the news, Mr. Paige came home really early in the morning, after having too much to drink and after the bars had closed. This wasn't out of the ordinary, apparently. Mary and I have had extensive conversations at the grocery store when we run into each other. Well, not extensive, I guess. But as extensive as you can be at the grocery store." She began rambling.

"Mom, please," I pleaded. She continued.

"She usually would just let me know how she and Ann were doing and eventually she would mention Alan and their problems. I, of course, would help in whatever way I could. I felt horrible, of course, because I don't have any experience with this sort of situation. Anyway, according to the police report, Mr. Paige came into the house at around 2:30 and woke up the girls by screaming at Mary. From what the neighbors heard, she was supposed to have picked Alan up from the bar at 1:00 but never did. From what I've heard around town and the neighbors, the scene played out a lot like it does in the movies. Mary started to cry, and Alan kept getting louder and angrier. Ann attempted to intervene, so Alan got a little too physical and that is when he hit Mary. He didn't hit her that hard, but it didn't matter when she hit the corner of the island in the kitchen. He was completely out of his mind and probably didn't ever really register what happened seeing as he was mostly running on alcohol. After he hit Mary, he went for Ann. She didn't pass out and he wouldn't stop hitting her. The neighbors called after they heard the first gunshot and since the police station is right down the road they were able to get there fairly fast, call for an ambulance, and break up the situation, but it seemed like things were too late."

My mom shifted in her seat while she took a pause from the gruesome story. I couldn't form a coherent thought. She continued quietly.

"Both Mary and Ann were rushed to the hospital and immediately treated for internal bleeding and concussions. Mary passed just this morning from the wound on her head and the internal bleeding caused by the gunshot. Ann still has not fully recovered, they said that the kind of beating she received is not something you ever fully recover from. She suffered too much blunt force trauma. The doctors have diagnosed her to be in a limbo state that could go pretty much any which way. When the original news story aired that following morning, it incorrectly reported both of their deaths."

I sat there in complete silence for a long time. *What if I had picked her up when she called me that morning?* I thought. I looked out of my hospital window as the rain continued to poor on the innocent victims only a few stories below. My mother embraced the silence along with me, hoping to feel some of the same feelings as me.

After a very long time I finally broke the silence with my one-word question.

"How?"

"What do you mean, honey?"

"I mean, how?"

"How what?"

"How could this have happened?"

"It wasn't completely unexpected, love. Mary and Ann needed to get out of that household for a long time and they didn't make it out in time. There are evil people in this world who don't understand what they are doing a lot of the time. In this case, that evil rested inside Mr. Paige. All we can do now is pray for Ann, Mary, and Mr. Paige's soul."

"..."

"I know this is really hard on you baby, but there is not much we can do to fix it."

"But she isn't gone?"

"Physically, she is not gone. But her mental state has deteriorated almost completely. There isn't much time left."

I immediately got up to leave but felt the intense pain where my rib cage was supposed to be completely intact. As soon as I started to get up *another* doctor came in with an official clipboard.

"Oh no, you don't, little man." *Little Man?* "You aren't gonna be getting up for a little while. After that car accident of yours, you are lucky to be alive and even this much intact. We need to put you on watch for the next few days."

"I'm sorry, but I need to visit my friend, she is much more important than my stupid injuries."

"I know, bud, however, you need to wait a few more hours. It's not best to have you go so quickly." *Bud?* I was a little relieved that I could at least see her in a few hours but also frustrated because I needed to see her now. The doctor told me to calm down and push my pain pump button next to my bed to relieve some of the pain. He also reassured me that I would be able to get where I needed to be soon enough. As if he knew where that was.

It was hell to sit in the same building as her but be so far away at the same time. I didn't sleep again, and I didn't turn on the TV as my mom suggested, I laid there sorting out the puzzle that was the past few days. It was slowly starting to piece itself together and become less fuzzy. As I pieced together the confusion, I experienced the familiar quiet waiting. I could tell my mom was experiencing it, too. She had resorted to the in-room magazines to occupy her time. She did the same thing at Dr. Sawyer's office years ago. At some point, while I continued to struggle with the concept of the past few days and as I struggled to fight off the quiet waiting, the unofficial paranoid practitioner came back in, still clipboard-less.

"Blake," he said, not asking.

"Who are you?" I finally asked, annoyed with the games that this hospital was playing.

"I am Dr. Sanjay, one of the psychologists on staff here." He pulled a stool up next to my bed and asked my mom for a few minutes alone. Of course, my mom agreed.

"Of course, Doctor. I'll be right outside the door if you need me." I didn't know if she was talking to me or the doctor when she said that last part. We both ended up nodding as she closed the door on her way out.

"So, am I going crazy?" I asked.

"We never like to use the word crazy."

"Okay, delusional than."

"You may have been delusional, but I still don't think that is the best term."

"What happened then? Why was she with me in the car? Why did it feel so real?"

"I am fairly confident to give the blame to a relapse of grief."

"Jesus, what a cop out. Grief?" *This guy was pissing me off.*

"I see here in my notes that you made a significant amount of progress with your previous psychologist Dr. Sawyer. Yes?"

"I guess. If by progress you mean I don't see my dead dad in places that he obviously is not. If so, yeah, I made a ton of progress. I have progress to spare."

"Well, in your sessions with Dr. Sawyer, I'm sure she had used the phrase: extraordinary experience?"

"Yeah, rings a bell."

"I believe you have begun to have these extraordinary experiences again."

"So, I am crazy."

"No, Blake, you are in mourning. That is a very different prognosis. When you saw the news of Ann and her mother's death on the news, your extraordinary experience took over and created this new reality for you to cope. This is not uncommon. Besides, if you were crazy, we wouldn't have kept you in this wing of the hospital and it is a belief that crazy people won't admit to being crazy."

"I guess I see where your logic is, but it doesn't make it less embarrassing for me." Dr. Sanjay just stared at me after saying this. I continued so as not to let the silence become too deafening. "I guess embarrassing may not be the right word. I honestly don't know what to call it. Confused perhaps? It just...it felt so real. Then to find out it was not, is just a lot to handle I guess. I don't know." He didn't respond. He just watched me. This definitely did not help with my mental state. I felt like an animal in the zoo that was being studied. Eventually he did speak, and I was whisked back from the zoo and into the Middleton Hospital once more.

"This is not uncommon, and you should not feel incompetent. In fact, I think you might be okay to go and see her now if you want. It could help your brain restructure the proper reality around yourself. I'll accompany you over to her room. It might help you process everything." I nodded.

Dr. Sanjay and I made our way to Ann's room. It was down a few different hallways, but the walk didn't take too long. However, it felt like hours because I wasn't sure what I expected to see. Last time I was put in this type of situation my grandmother was fighting a losing battle with leukemia. She eventually went into a comatose state and passed just after we all said our goodbyes. I looked over at Dr. Sanjay while we walked.

"You know, last time I saw someone who was in a vegetable type mindset, they passed away immediately after talking to them. I think I might be bad luck and Ann doesn't deserve that from me."

He just forced a chuckle and said, "You'll be fine, Blake. Believe it or not, you can't talk someone to death. Some of the nurses here, however, probably could pull that off." I found myself sort of liking Dr. Sanjay. After a few moments, he stopped at what I could only assume was her room. "Blake," he started, "you need to go in there confident and as yourself. There are many doctors, including myself, who believe that a comatose patient is fully aware of what is being said to them and done to them, they just cannot do anything about it. So again, be yourself and just talk to her." He opened the door and wheeled me inside.

I'd love to say that I kept my composure for Ann. I'd love to say that everything in that moment made sense in the world. I'd love to say that I was able to craft together the perfect thing to say to her seeing as it may have been my last time with her. But, I didn't do any of those things. The minute I saw her laying in the hospital bed hooked up to an infinite number of machines, the world around me shattered. Aliens who may have been orbiting the earth would have heard the shattering of my heart, yet again, as Ann tore it asunder. Here was this beautiful and remarkable girl whom, I believed, to be invincible, and she was at her weakest. She was vulnerable and dying. She wasn't the same Ann that knocked on my door the day she moved in down the street. She wasn't the same Ann that I had grown up with. She wasn't the same Ann that I had admired for putting the post-it notes around the school. She wasn't the same Ann that called me weeks earlier asking me if I wanted to go skydiving. She certainly wasn't the same Ann that I had made up who had whisked me away on an adventure. The same one who slept in a tent with me and who helped me find H. Jackson Brown. She was a completely different being in that bed: a total stranger. Dr. Sanjay interrupted my silent mourning.

"Blake?"

"..."

"I know how hard this is for you."

"..."

"You don't have to stay in here."

"..."

"We can go now if you want to."

"No."

"Excuse me?"

"I need to stay. But I need to stay by myself."

He wouldn't let me stay in there by myself. He said something about my lack of psychological stability. So, we left. I left without looking back at her because Dr. Sanjay made it clear to me that the stranger in the bed wasn't Ann. It wouldn't be Ann ever again. He explained that even if she fully recovers, she will never be the same. Eventually, I made it back into my hospital room, fell asleep, and became susceptible to my normal nightmare.

I awoke in my room back home in an empty bed yet again unclothed and exposed. My closet was still empty and the curtains around my window still remained unmovable. I still felt uneasy as I made my way around the house. Eventually, like last time, I was washed in the desire to find Ann and found myself making my way outside again. I felt the drab lack of temperature and sunlight and made my way towards her house. Like the last time I was here, the sidewalks were empty of pedestrians and the streets lacked cars. However, across the street from me on the opposite sidewalk there was a wheelchair. I knew that it was not meant for me and there was no one sitting in it. Instead, there sat a handgun. After instinctively checking the road for passing cars, I jogged towards the wheel chair, grabbing it and pushing it along as I continued my journey towards Ann's house. The scream came from behind me and this time I was ready for it. Both the wheelchair and I approached the faceless man wearing the military uniform. The man spoke once more. "If it's not a beautiful morning, let cheerfulness make it one." I made it closer to the man but this time he took a step back. It seemed as if he was fearful of me. Every step that I took with the wheel chair towards him, he would take two steps away from me. We continued like this until he was out of sight and I turned back towards my goal.

Ann's house was exactly where it had been for the many years that I had known her. It was as charming and inviting as it had always been. I tentatively walked towards the house and observed my surroundings. Ann's house was in fact the only part of the warped Middleton that looked like it belonged. As I looked at the familiar house, I was reminded about the importance of the skin. It hides all of the chaos of the inner body, similar to the architecture of a house. Just by looking at Ann's house, I was unable to see all of the terrible things that must have happened inside that house at the hands of Mr. Paige. It was only as I entered the house, did I finally see what had happened the night of the event. As soon as I pushed the wheelchair through the threshold, I could smell the trouble, the fear, and the blood. I made my way into the kitchen and was greeted by Mrs. Paige's limp body. She was laying on the floor as if she were asleep. Blood leaked from a large wound on her head. Her face held the ghost of despair and surprise that it must have emoted moments before she fell prey to her husband. I forced myself to look away and I walked through the kitchen, into the living room. There, Ann lay helplessly as blood leaked from her head from the blunt force trauma. She too held the ghost of despair and disappointment at her father's twisted actions. To see the woman I loved, unable to do anything but hold her wound and wait for help, was appalling. I looked around and saw Mr. Paige. He was asleep in the recliner with a drink in his hand. I stepped towards him while I began to clench my fists. He woke up and saw me approaching him.

"What are you doing in my house, boy?" he shouted.

"What have you done?" I continued to walk towards him.

"Get out!"

"You stole one of the most important people in my life," I replied quietly.

"I said get out!" I didn't listen.

"But you sit there with so much pride," I tightened my grip. "So much satisfaction. You are a sad, pathetic, and sick creature. You are a twisted human and a poor excuse for a father."

He spoke. "You don't understand what you are talking about, boy."

I continued. "Your daughter was the most amazing girl, and not only did you take her away from me, you took her away from this world. Now the world will never get to know the amazing person I had the pleasure of knowing. She wasn't some girl that I had observed from afar. She was someone I had the honor of knowing closely."

"She was nothing," he spat. I stopped and felt my hand tighten around something that was not my fist. When I looked down, I saw the handgun from the wheelchair. I had somehow procured it while I spoke. He saw it too, and his eyes widened. I held it up to his head and continued to speak.

"Now you, and only you, have taken that opportunity away from everyone else. You've destroyed more lives than just hers." Mr. Paige stood a foot away from me at this point. He was as real as Ann had been in the car ride to Nashville and to Catoosa. I felt myself slipping, but I couldn't stop. "If you aren't disturbed by your actions, then I need to use this gun and end it now. If for some miraculous reason you are slightly disturbed than I will never give you the satisfaction of putting you down like the animal you are. You are an absolute disgrace to the world that God accidentally put you in. I will never rest until I know that you are suffering from the worst things this world has to offer.

"Knowing our great, justice system, you'll eventually get out of the rat hole you call a cell and you'll be back on the street. You'll never be able to find a job because they won't hire an alcoholic convict who killed his family because he was too much of a coward to kill himself. You will wander from gutter to gutter looking for comfort that you will never find. On that glorious day, when your body finally shuts down, or you finally decide to put a bullet in your mouth, and do everyone a favor, I will be able to rest and feel like justice has been served. You will await your end with hope that the suffering will be over, but it will have only just begun. You will die with no one there to care about your death, and you will enter Hell and you will receive worse torture than your pathetic excuse for a brain could even imagine. You will rot there with the worst men in history who don't even compare to how twisted you are."

He didn't speak. Instead, he stared at me, waiting to see what I would do next. I didn't drop the gun, nor did I move it out of his face. He needed to feel the same way he made Ann and her mother feel: powerless. He needed to know that the only reason he was going to survive was by my own mercy and not by anything he had done. He needed to know.

"Go on and do it," he said, spitting on the floor. "I don't have any regret. In fact, I'd kill the bitch again." He stood up and put his own forehead to the barrel of the gun. "Do it!"

I awoke to the sound of the gunshot and was thrust from my delusion.

Twelve

After

I'm not exactly sure when I arrived home. As I collapsed onto my bed and let my sluggishness and fecklessness overtake me, I began to rethink the events that took place. When I said yes to her, I didn't think this would be the result. If I did, I never would have said yes. I would have politely told her no and continued on with my life. Things would have made much more sense if I only did that. If only I said no. I quickly fell asleep and met my dad again in my usual nightmare.

"Blake!" My mom rushed into my room yanking me from my meeting. She hugged me, and I longed for the cathartic comfort that she could provide. I needed someone to feel my pain. I needed someone to know how much I was hurting and who better than my mom. After so much confusion and not knowing what was real, I knew she was and she would always be. I understand now that I never should take my mom for granted. She will always be there for me, even when no one else is.

"Has the date been decided yet?" I asked tentatively.

"No, honey, the family is still grieving, and everything is being figured out. I am sure it will be sometime this week, but you don't have to go if you don't want -"

"No!" I interrupted her. "I need to go, it's a final goodbye." My mom shook her head as she hugged me again. "I need to go." I repeated to myself.

"They might hold out a little to see if Ann recovers. If not, I'm sure they will have a double burial and service. I think Mary and Ann would like that." I simply nodded.

I just laid in bed for most of the next day. I had already called in sick to work. My boss seemed to understand before I was able to come up with an excuse as to why I was calling in. *Why didn't I just tell her the truth?* I was completely broken; physically, mentally, and emotionally. I wasn't able to sleep after the few hours I got the night before, because images of the previous day kept swimming in my mind every time I closed my eyes. I thought of the doctors standing there and telling my mom what had happened. I remember waiting to go home. I remembered previous days as well, like the car ride to Nashville that felt like an eternity. How idiotic of me to compare those few hours in the car as an eternity. The true eternity was the few minutes that I spent awake the previous night in between nightmares. But I couldn't just stop living. I wouldn't allow my nightmares to become reality, I would continue to live and continue to be the new me: The me I was introduced to by her.

At one point during my anguished brooding, my appetite came back. It arrived as slyly as a tsunami arrives during high tides. Unlike everything else around me, it was not something that I could simply ignore. I headed downstairs to the kitchen and passed my mom who was surprised to see me up and about.

"Oh, hey, honey! Where are you headed?"

"I'm just getting something to eat. I'm gonna head back upstairs as soon as I get something." She seemed kind of sad and a little frustrated with me. I couldn't blame her.

"Oh, okay. Well, if you need anything, just know –"

"I know, mom, you're there," I interrupted. She left me to my mission and understood that the hostility was not something that was intended. She knew, after years of grieving my dad's death, what grieving all entails. It was something no one wants to be an expert about.

When you are grieving, your mind forgets very normal things. For example, as I was attempting to make cereal to silence my angry stomach, I put the milk in the pantry not thinking twice. I only realized it when I was trying to put my cereal away in the refrigerator. It is interesting how human minds react to different events or situations in their lives. Yet, when you are put in a dangerous situation, adrenaline kicks in and you are able to perform crazy and superhuman actions. Grief affects you differently as well. Your mind is so focused on the grief and that sadness, that it has a hard time focusing on the normal things that we think about such as the preferred temperature of milk. Our mind is interesting. Brown tells us, "Be tough minded and tenderhearted." However, during grief, we can only be tenderhearted because our mind is not tough enough to handle the pain.

I often sat alone, mulling over my condition. I think my mom realized that I needed the company if I was ever going to recover emotionally or psychologically, because she called the Halls. This became obvious to me when Ian texted me.

Ian (2:47 P.M.): *Hey! My family is going to head back home for a few days. I hope I'm able to come hang out with you for a bit! Lemme know.*

Me (4:30 P.M.): *Hey dude, sorry I didn't have my phone on me. That would be great. When do you guys think you'll head back?*

Ian (4:32 P.M.): *Don't worry about it. We were going to leave probably tomorrow morning if that works for you. Meet up for lunch?*

Me (4:34 P.M.): *Yeah sure, where do you want to meet up?*

Ian (4:35 P.M.): *The usual place?*

Me (4:37 P.M.): *Definitely. Lemme know when you get here, and I'll head over.*

When Ian and I were still close and we both still lived in Middleton, we would always hang out at the small café down the street from my house. In fact, it was the only restaurant in

Middleton. Despite this, however, we enjoyed our little trips to the café. We would spend any allowance or small cash that we had as kids, at the café, on consumable items that were savored for no longer than ten minutes. He texted me the next day around 11:30 in the morning, to inform me of his arrival. I got up from my nest of a bed, showered, and grabbed clothes. He was waiting for me at the café when I arrived at 11:45.

"Hey, buddy. I'm glad we were able to meet up!" He stood up to give me a hug, which I accepted.

"Where are your parents?"

"Oh, they went to go meet up with Mrs. Wong. I think she is trying to get my parent's pizza dough recipe." He laughed and took a sip of his water. "What's new with you?" he asked, attempting to ignite the conversation.

"It's just hard," I said plainly. He nodded. It was apparent to me that he heard what had happened. I assumed my mom had filled them in and warned them about any symptoms that may reveal themselves. *Of course, it's important to monitor the mad man.* I thought. I spoke again before Ian could try to comfort me. "I heard about what happened in the hospital. My mom told me."

"Yeah? How do you feel?" Ian asked cautiously.

"I'm not crazy, if that's what you're wondering," I said a little too harsh.

"That's not what I meant, dude."

"I know, I'm sorry. I'm doing alright. I wasn't even that beat up by the accident. The hospital thought it best to keep me on psychiatric watch." An awkward silence filled the gap between us after I said this. I could tell Ian felt uncomfortable. Ignoring the discomfort, I looked around at the café. Familiar faces were sitting around us and continued to glance in mine and Ian's direction. It was obvious why they were paying attention to us. Bailey Bremer and her boyfriend sat just two tables away from us and ceased all conversation since we sat down. Instead, they gazed upon us in waiting. A few other familiar faces had done the same thing while they waited.

"What are they waiting for?" I asked Ian, not very quietly.

"Don't worry about them, bud. You know that everyone in Middleton will soak up whatever drama or gossip is thrown at them." Ian was always good at trying to make me feel better, no matter the circumstance. "They're a bunch of savages," he added, loud enough so everyone could hear. This seemed to get their attention and they at least started acting like they were having their own conversations, instead of prying into ours. "What have you been up to?" Ian asked, attempting to steer the conversation away from psychiatric problems.

"Honestly?" I asked him.

"Sure."

"Nothing. I've just been thinking about the past couple of days, trying to piece together the holes." It was obvious to Ian that the subject of my past week was not something that could be easily dropped. Ian, however, was saved with trying to console me even more, as a mutual friend from school approached us.

"Hey, what's going on, Garrett." Ian said, standing up to shake his hand. It was ignored.

"I…uh…I heard what happened, Blake." It was not clear whether Garrett was mocking me or attempting sympathy. Either way, it came off as rude.

"Yeah, and I suppose you're waiting for me to lose it again. Is that it?" I shot at him, equally as rude.

"No. I'm sorry. I'm not trying to suggest anything. I guess I just wanted to say that I'm here." I didn't respond. "You know, if you need anything," he added, clearly intimidated by my candor.

"Gee, thanks. That's so kind. I'll make sure to take you up on that offer." I scorned. He walked away, and it was clear that was not how he wanted the situation to transpire. Ian sat back down and sat their quietly, obviously intimidated as well.

"I know, I know. He was just trying to help," I told him, moderately confessing my fault.

"I'm not gonna say anything," he said simply. "Everyone has their own way to deal with stuff. Yours, doesn't line up with Garrett's, it seems."

"So, it would seem," I responded. There was another lull in conversation while we sat in the café. I began to rethink the nightmare that I had in the hospital and felt it was time to confess my rage. "I killed him." Ian was understandably taken aback by this statement. He set his water down and his eyes grew wide and worrisome.

"You what?"

"In a dream, I mean."

"Oh. Mr. Paige?" he inquired.

"Yeah. I've been having the same nightmarish dream for the past few days. It always starts with me being naked in my room. I'm unable to find clothes, so I just leave my house."

"You never have been a prude," Ian joked. I ignored it.

"I walk around Middleton, looking for Ann. Instead, I find my dad." I paused, waiting to hear Ian's response. He must not have known how to approach the subject, so I continued. "He quotes H. Jackson Brown to me and then leaves. Eventually, I find her house. Up until the last night in hospital, I always woke up before I made it inside. That night, however, I made it inside and saw what happened." This time Ian spoke.

"What do you mean?"

"I mean, I saw it. I saw Mrs. Paige on the floor. I saw Ann with her bullet wound. I saw Mr. Paige, drinking and looking at his handiwork."

"Geez, dude. That's dark," Ian said, clearly disturbed. I didn't spare him any details.

"I kill him, I think." I told him.

"You think?" He was confused.

"Yeah, every time that I have the dream, I wake up to the gunshot."

Silence ensued.

"Maybe you die?" he said finally.

"Huh?"

"Maybe you die," he repeated. "People always say that you wake up when you die in a dream. Maybe you wake up because you die." I took a second to think.

"I never thought about it. I guess that would make sense, though."

"Do you say anything to him before you wake up?" Ian questioned.

"Yeah, I let him have it. Basically, I go to sleep incredibly angry and wake up feeling like I released my anger in my sleep."

"I guess that's the best way to do it. It beats you taking it out on me," he chuckled.

"That's still a possibility." I joked back.

"I think it was Richard Emerson who said, 'For every minute you remain angry you give up a minute of peace of mind." I smiled as Ian attempted the Emerson quote.

"It was Ralph Emerson who said it. He said, 'For every minute you remain angry, you give up sixty seconds of peace of mind.'"

Ian nodded. "Yeah, that's what I meant. Now, do you want to go play videogames and try to get your mind off all this for a little bit?"

"Hell yeah," I said as we both got up from our table and headed out of the café.

Thirteen

After

Neither of us held onto our Slash like abilities while playing *Guitar Hero*. We started out over confident on expert difficulty and throughout the night slowly worked our way down to medium difficulty. I found myself giggling at a few of his jokes and continued to appreciate my best friend again. Into the late night, we were both extremely tired and I began talking to him about my experience in Nashville and Catoosa. He seemed nervous as I started talking about it. I told him about talking to Rosemary and Brown. I told him about the absurd desire to learn about this quote. Ian, of course, supported me all the same. Things were back to normal as we started talking.

Him: Well, did you find out who officially said it? I mean you talked to Brown…

Me: Right. Which was amazing but as humbled as he was he told us there was no reason we shouldn't go research the other side of the argument.

Him: Damn, this guy sounds kinda edgy.

Me: Yeah, I know but he does have a point. Even if he never said the quote, Brown was all about throwing off the bowlines, maybe this was his way of telling us to do so.

There was a slight pause after I had finished that statement, and I wasn't sure why. Ian broke the awkward silence after a few moments. "…it was his way of telling *you* to do so." I let that sink in for a few minutes. I sat there and reflected what I had said. I still didn't quite understand the episode, but I knew it had happened. Things were silent too long and Ian stepped up yet again.

Him: Let's go.

Me: Go where?

Him: To Missouri. Let's find a Mark Twain expert and talk to him.

Me: An expert? On Mark Twain?

Him: Yeah, like someone who is as obsessed with Twain as you are with this Brown guy.

Me: Whoa, I'm not obsessed, I just appreciate his work.

Him: Okay, whatever.

We looked at each other and started to violently nod our heads. "Hell yeah," we both said. So, we got to planning. We put together Ian's cash and my credit card and we packed up ready to leave in the morning. This time, I would be able to talk to my mom and tell her where I was going. This time, I would be able to prepare for a road trip. This time, I wouldn't go alone.

In the morning, we started to pack Ian's car. He talked to his parent's earlier the night before and asked if it was okay that he take the car for the day to Hannibal. They agreed it would be fine if it made me feel better. He went and picked up the car as I woke up my mom and told her the plan.

"Mom, I know you probably aren't going to be too psyched about this, but Ian and I are going to Missouri." I waited for her to yell. I waited for her to mention the car accident. I waited for her to ask about our transportation. I even half waited for her to smack me on the head to try and "knock some sense into me." She took a breath in before she addressed the situation. I knew that she didn't want me to go, but I also sensed that she understood the situation and maybe even the urgency. The doctors had filled her in about my trip to Tennessee, so there wasn't much for me to say.

"Is this about her?" She said it calmly and slightly broken. I nodded my head and she took another breath.

"I owe it to her, Mom. I know she isn't gone, but if I am able to give her good news before she passes, I will have done everything in my power to help her." I teared up as I said this.

"I know I don't have to remind you about anything from the past week. The only thing I have to say is be safe and be smart." I hugged her, thanked her, and promised her that we would be safe.

As Ian and I were making our way out of the driveway in his car, I looked over at my mom and saw her waving us goodbye with a look of concern on her face. I understood where she was coming from, but something felt different about this road trip. Any thought of apprehension was left back in the house. We couldn't afford to take any of that with us this time around. This time, something just felt right. We were supposed to go to Missouri. We were supposed to go and figure out who said this stupid quote. It's not even about who said it. At that point, I didn't give a damn who said it, as long as I found out. Not for me, not for Ian, but for her.

We had to jump on I-55 to get to Missouri and it took us a little bit to get going in the right direction. We did not waver in our resolve. We stayed dedicated to the cause and to the mission. We were ready for this. I had my best friend back and we were even going to try and have fun with this. We turned up the radio and we drove.

We stopped for gas station food in the smaller university town of Cape Girardeau, Missouri. We had only been driving for a couple hours, but we skipped breakfast and we were hungry. I quickly ran into the gas station and found my way to the restroom. My earlier gas station restroom hypothesis and conclusion was proven again by the grotesquely cylindrical basin. I washed my hands quickly and headed towards the grill to find a snack. I settled on a roller filled with processed meat and egg that was all conveniently wrapped in a tortilla. Ian got the same. We approached the counter so as to check out.

"So, that'll be 2 breakfast wraps. Anything else?"

"No ma'am that'll be it," I said as I reached for my wallet. Ian slapped my hand and pulled out his own.

"You've been through enough, buddy. I'll take care of this. Besides, my dad is paying for it." I laughed as he used *his* emergency credit card to pay.

"How much longer until we get to Hannibal?" I questioned as I buckled my seatbelt and Ian started the car.

"If we continue on 55, we have a little longer than 3 hours. We are making decent time. So, I can probably get us there in about 3 hours." He pulled out of the gas station and made his way back towards I-55 North.

"Just drive safe. I really don't feel like getting into another accident after everything I've been through."

"That's fair." He pushed on the gas and the engine revved as it reached about 4 miles over the speed limit of 70 mph.

"It felt so real," I said with my voice cracking as he turned on the cruise control. I watched the billboards pan through my vision but looked toward the horizon, not focusing on any particular advertisement. I could hear the uncomfortable silence coming from Ian. Although I wanted it to cease, I felt it calming somehow. It was terrible for me to think but I liked that he had a small sense of what I experienced during my episode. In the end, he did break the silence.

"I know, buddy. But it wasn't, and you can't really make it real." We sat there in silence again for a few seconds before I spoke once more.

"I just don't know how to describe it. I don't know how I didn't pick up on the clues that this might not seem real."

A beat.

"I think the biggest clue you overlooked was that you couldn't possibly land Ann in a million years." We both laughed and that helped to expel some of the awkwardness that existed between the passenger and driver's seat.

"Is it okay if I turn on the radio again?" Ian asked reaching for the knob.

"Of course, as long as you turn on something good."

Ian began flipping through some channels and we heard brief segments of different songs being broadcasted to parts of Missouri. "– is a burning thing and it makes a – respirar tu cuello despacito. Deja que – listening to 103.5 your R&B radio – love me, oh didn't I, didn't I, didn't I see you cryin' – chew tobacco, chew tobacco – SUNDAY, SUNDAY, SUNDAY!" As the songs and stationed flipped, I was reminded of how Ann would change my radio station as if she owned the vehicle when she was in the passenger seat. I wanted her to do this again.

After searching for something to listen to, we eventually made it back full circle to Cheap Trick's *I want you to want me* and just left it on. The song finished almost immediately after we made it back to it and its end triggered a string of radio ads. Ian and I didn't have very much to say to each other, so we didn't speak, however it was not awkward. There was no obligation to spark up conversation between us and that was okay. The radio ads soon ended and the silence and lack of speaking quickly evaporated, as a new song came on the radio. It is an incredibly cliché road trip song, so we were very thankful that it began to play seeing as we were not musically prepared to take on the trip to Hannibal. Not only was it cliché but it did mean a lot to us and it was sort of a foundation in mine and Ian's friendship when we were on a class field trip in sixth-grade.

We went to a land fill as a sixth-grade class to learn about decomposition and to help implement this "Go Green" initiative that the school board was pushing pretty hard. The nearest land fill from Middleton wasn't too far off; but it was a decent drive via school bus and screaming sixth graders. I sat in the back in an attempt to limit any contact with the other students. Ian had the same idea but the only open seat in the back was next to me, so he sat down. It was a little awkward to start with neither of us saying anything. I glanced over at him with annoyance because he sat next to me, but it wasn't his fault. I know that now. Silently and irritably, I scooted closer to the window of the bus as far as I could, taking my backpack with me. Eventually he broke the silence.

"Hey…"

"Hi."

"Aren't you in Ms. Calhoun's advisory class?"

"Uh, yeah."

"…"

"Are you?"

"Yeah, I actually just had to move in there because I was having problems with another kid in my class, Brett."

I nodded in response to his relocation to my advisory class and stared back out the window and eventually put in my headphones, to listen to my (yes this was almost seven years ago) iPod shuffle.

I shook my iPod to shuffle and began looking out of the window of the bus as we headed onto the highway. By fate, the song Bohemian Rhapsody by Queen started up and my mental music video film began to roll. I was just starting to hear Freddy Mercury sing "Momma...just killed a man," when Ian yanked out one of my ear buds. I paused the song and turned to him.

"What the hell, man?" I said angrily.

"Dude, is that Queen?"

"Yeah. It's Boh- "

"-hemian Rhapsody. Yeah, I know! That is totally sick. I love Queen."

"I'm not the biggest fan, but yeah their music is pretty decent." I shrugged.

Ian just kept staring at me waiting for me to pick up on the social cue that he was laying down. However, as he would soon learn as my best friend: I am terrible at picking up social cues. He spoke again.

"Do you mind if I listen with you? I didn't think to bring my mp3 player." I reluctantly agreed and handed him my other earbud, so we could listen together. After listening to a few of the songs from *The Greatest Hits of Queen*, he shuffled the music over to my most embarrassing playlist which I titled; *Nsync vs. Backstreet Boys.*

"No way!" Ian started to say.

"Don't make fun of me, dude. My mom uses this iPod sometimes," I lied.

"Oh, I was about to get really excited."

"Wait…you were?" I said confused.

"Yeah, but it's no contest."

"What do you mean?" I asked.

"Nsync," he said confidently.

"Nsync?" I repeated like an idiot.

"Yeah, dude. Nsync. Screw the Backstreet Boys, Nsync all the way."

And that was it. "Screw Backstreet Boys, Nsync all the way," was the exact phrase when I realized this is someone I could become best friends with. For the rest of the bus ride to the land fill, we trash talked the Backstreet Boys.

He said things like, "*I want it that way* and *The Call* are the only truly noteworthy Backstreet Boys songs."

I replied with things like, "Oh my God, dude, right? Like, I get that the Backstreet Boys were around first, but Nsync was just essentially a much better version. I mean, nobody goes around and raves about how good the *Rat Pack* was in the original *Oceans 11* movie from the '60s." I caught myself with the previous analogy. "Well, I guess that is not a good analogy because I would never compare Nick Carter to Sinatra. However, I would put Timberlake and Damon on the same level playing field." Ian and I laughed and would continue to laugh for the next six years. It was that same laughter that would carry our story back into the car on the way to Hannibal.

"...anywhere the wind blows." We sang out the last lines almost as delicately as Freddy Mercury, applauded, and continued our laughter. We let the car radio act as our DJ as we drove the road less traveled and reached our Twainian destination.

"Well, Hannibal certainly is charming," Ian said, pulling onto S. Main Street and parking a few blocks down from the Mark Twain Hotel. "I would suggest going to the Mark Twain museum and speaking with a curator about the quote." I agreed and followed Ian to a nearby map of downtown to see if a museum was labeled. In fact, there were a few different museums located in town. The nearest one was the childhood home of Mark Twain, so we decided to pursue our inquiries there. "Are you okay with walking? I'd rather not jump in the car for a trip just a few blocks away."

"Absolutely, I need the fresh air," I responded.

I had to agree with Ian, Hannibal was indeed very charming. From the names of the hotels to the attractions pointing to the riverfront, charisma filled the sidewalks. Hannibal was a place that anyone could find themselves discovering a creative outlet like Twain did. As we walked down S. Main Street and through the town square, we admired the inviting atmosphere. Even more so, we admired the exterior of the boyhood home of Mark Twain. Oddly enough, the house was on a substantial incline and it appeared the house was crooked. Ian and I, knowing this was a just a trick of the eye, did not let it bother us greatly. While we reveled in the solidity of the home, we were quickly greeted by who I could only assume to be the curator.

"Good afternoon!" A portly, middle-aged man came stomping down the slight decline to shake our hands. He was wearing khakis, suspenders, oversized shoes, and attempted to work a handlebar mustache. "It's good to have some visitors. What are ya'll here to see?" This new man's enthusiasm, attire, and flamboyancy was a lot to handle at once.

"Uhm, we aren't really sure what we are looking for, yet. I guess we're just browsing." The man did not miss a beat to respond to me.

"Hey! That's okay, let me show you around in Mark Twain's old house. Maybe you will find some inspiration." Ian gave me a puzzled look as we followed the curator into the house. "My name's Pete by the way."

This time Ian spoke in response. "I'm Ian and this is Blake. We are here wanting to learn a little bit about Mark Twain and his childhood. It would also be great if we found some answers to a few questions that we have," Pete's enthusiasm continued.

"Well, I'll be more than willing to help with what I can. To start our tour, I'd like to tell you about a man name Samuel Clemens…" Pete started his educational tour by allowing us to finish our examination of the exterior of the house while he revealed to us the (not so) shocking revelation of Mark Twain's real name: Samuel Clemens. He then continued at the origins of the home. "In 1843, Sam moved into this home. He lived here until about 1853." Before continuing up the significant incline to the house, he pointed out the white picket fence out front. "This, as you may be able to tell from the sign, is Tom Sawyer's Fence. I'm sure you know what fence the sign is referring to in Mark Twain's *The Adventures of Tom Sawyer.*" Ian spoke.

"I've actually never read *Tom Sawyer*; however, I do know that in the novel Tom Sawyer tricks somebody to paint a fence, so he doesn't have to. Is that correct, Pete?" Pete seemed disappointed in his lack of experience with Mark Twain.

"Yes, that is correct."

Ian spoke again, "Why does he trick the kid? Why not just do the work?"

"Why don't I answer this question by providing Twain's own analysis within the story." Pete then began to quote a section directly out of *The Adventures of Tom Sawyer.*

"Tom said to himself that it was not such a hollow world, after all. He had discovered a great law of human action, without knowing it – namely, that in order to make a man or a boy covet a thing, it is only necessary to make the thing difficult to attain. If he had been a great and wise philosopher, like the writer of this book, he would now have comprehended that Work consists of whatever a body is obliged to do, and that Play consists of whatever a body is not obliged to do." Pete stopped and waited for our absent applause. *How Ann-esque.* I thought.

We continued our tour up the incline and towards the front door. Pete stopped at the top of the hill and in front of the door and began wheezing. It was obvious that he didn't see enough visitors to venture out of his office and greet them down the vast downward slope. He used the door for support while he caught his breath.

"Do you get many visitors?" Ian asked politely.

"No sir, most everyone around these parts have been to the house plenty of times. Surprisingly enough, Hannibal doesn't get too many visitors looking to hear about good old Sam. Why don't I show you inside?"

The inside was as compact as the outside made it look. There were a lot of labels in and around each room to help the tour guide and to help us locate what was being discussed. Pete, however, didn't defer to the labels and seemed to go off-script. All in all, the most notable collections that were shown to us in the museum were Twain's old typewriter, Twain's writing desk and chair, as well as his famous white jacket which he is usually depicted wearing.

"This jacket is believed to be the only one in existence," Pete said with an uncomfortable amount of excitement.

Observation: Pete seems like the kind of guy who would get very bored sitting in a house that no one visits all day.

Analysis on Observation: I wouldn't be surprised if he walks around wearing the endangered jacket.

Conclusion: Poor Pete.

In the museum, there were many busts made in Twain's image. This was slightly unsettling, and it created an aura of judgement against us. I examined one of the busts from his older years. His mustache was prodigious, his brow was furrowed, and he looked to be in a concentrated thought. I wondered if this was the thought of a man who conjured up the quote which has motivated and consumed my mind. Near the busts of Twain, there was a wide collection of original letters by Twain himself. Pete must have seen me looking at the letters.

"There are more than 60 original Mark Twain letters here at the museum. They are correspondences between his wife, his children, and even a few between Sam and Tom Blankenship."

"Who is Tom Blankenship?" I inquired.

"It's believed that Tom was the model for –"

I interrupted him. "Tom Sawyer?"

He took his verbal control back. "Actually no. Tom Blankenship is believed to have been the inspiration for Huckleberry Finn."

I nodded to express my understanding and my unwillingness to hear more. All in all, the tour at the Hermitage back in Nashville with Ian was slightly more exciting than Twain's childhood home. I was also lacking an answer to my still trivial question. Ian realized that I was frustrated so he stepped up.

"Excuse me, Pete? I have a question regarding a quote by Twain." Pete perked up, feeling wanted.

"Of course, lay it on me."

"Twenty years from now you will be more disappointed by the things you didn't do than by the ones you did do. So, throw off the bowlines…" Ian stopped and tried to figure out the rest of the quote. I helped, repeating where he had left off.

"So, throw off the bowlines, sail away from the safe harbor, catch the trade winds in your sails. Explore. Dream. Discover." We stood there quietly while Pete looked at us curiously.

"Twain said many quotes in his life and is often misquoted. I am pretty sure Twain did not say this particular quote. He did, however say, in *Following the Equator*, 'It is my belief that nearly any invented quotation played with confidence, stands a good chance to deceive.'" I had still received no definite answer. We thanked Pete for his time and his tour and headed out of the museum just as my next episode began.

I saw her sitting in the room with all of the letters and the bust that I had examined earlier.

"This man is pretty wrinkled," she said, nodding towards Twain.

"Wrinkles should merely indicate where the smiles have been," I said, quoting someone whom I had forgotten.

"How are you doing?" she asked, reaching for my hand.

"I miss you," I said truthfully. There was no point in lying to her. She wasn't even physically gone yet, and I already missed her.

"I don't have much time left. If you need to say goodbye, you should do it soon."

I felt Ian grab my arm and I was immediately whisked back into reality.

"Is it happening again?" he asked as he led me out of the house. We passed a sign on our way out of famous Twain quotes and one in particular caught my attention. It read: "Don't part with your illusions. When they are gone you may still exist, but you have ceased to live." Not for the first time, I completely disagreed with Twain.

Fourteen

After

Thanks to me, our trip to Hannibal was cut short. Ian drove all evening to get us back to Middleton and didn't mind the fact that I wasn't in the mood to talk. I told him about my brief encounter with her at the museum and he decided that it would be best to get back home to my mom and Dr. Sanjay.

Ian dropped me off at my house only after I had promised to keep him updated about everything going on. He said his parents were headed into town to visit with everyone and he would meet up with them. "Thank you for everything, Ian. Thanks for Nashville, thanks for sticking up for me and keeping me cool at the café. Also, thanks for taking me to Hannibal. You are a true friend, and I hope I can be the same to you someday." He smiled at me and gave me an awkward car hug.

"I love you, bud. You are a great friend to me and you travelled all the way to Nashville just to see me. I appreciate you, and who knows, maybe we'll end up at the same college." I agreed that we would keep each other updated more than we have the past few years and he drove off out of sight.

My mom immediately came out of the house, car keys in hand, and ready to go. "Where are you going?" I asked concerned.

"We need to get down to the hospital. They don't think she's going to make it through the night."

Heraclitus of Ephesus once said, "Time is a game played beautifully by children." If this is true, and time is a game, I want to stop playing.

I built my relationship with Ann the same way that someone would build a fire. You start with a small spark and begin growing it, little by little, until you eventually throw in everything you have. But now, this fire has consumed me and there is no way to stop the fire from the inside. Occasionally, there are wildfires that cannot be stopped by any amount of resistance. In those cases, the only thing that can be done is to contain the fire and wait for it to burn up by itself. This is one of those cases. As I looked at Ann, I felt the nonverbal decision to contain this fire and allow it to burn up. I looked at Ann and I felt the flames roar higher and hotter. I looked at Ann as longingly as I always had. I began to study every one of her features so as not to forget.

I studied what I remembered before Mr. Paige attempted to steal her beauty the same way he had stolen her life. He must have forgotten that Ann's beauty was not something that could be stolen. I studied her long brown hair which laid just below her shoulders. I studied her face and imagined where her blue eyes would be if her eyes were not closed. I studied her always visible dimples as well as the few freckles that always showed themselves in the summer sun. I studied the smallness of her nose which only accentuated the remaining features of her face. I studied her long neck and the softness of her small hands. I would never know what it would feel like to hold hands as two people who were mutually in love. She was as beautiful as she had always been without trying. This time, however, I was not longing for her affection but her time. I needed just a few more days, a few more weeks, and perhaps a few more lifetimes with her. This selfish wish would go un-granted just as most selfish wishes do. Before traveling outside of Middleton, Ann was the light of my small world and when I traveled, that light shone just as bright. My world grew and my love and admiration for Ann grew as well. No matter what Dr. Sanjay says, Ann was with me during that trip and she would be with me for the many other trips I will take. My light will continue to grow as my world would grow.

Seeing as Ann's mother had already passed away and was unable to be present for her final breaths, I was allowed to stay and hold her hand. Dr. Sanjay suggested my mother be there to help me deal with it and remind me of the true reality if I began to slip from it again. The doctors' jobs were not difficult. I grabbed Ann's hand and squeezed while my mom mimicked my actions on my own hand. I didn't really know how to feel as I watched the doctors begin to turn everything off. Of course, I cried, but other than that, I couldn't describe my emotions. I thought of the word, 'unreal' and then felt myself slipping. I squeezed my mom's hand and was brought back to reality.

The doctors finished their jobs and waited with my mom and I to see if their work was successful. It's a common cliché that when someone dies, they see their whole lives flash before their eyes. I was curious as to whether or not this was happening for Ann while we held her hand or if the images had come and gone on the night that her future was stolen away. In any state, a life did flash before *my* eyes while I held her there in the clean hospital room: ours. I saw myself gathering up the courage to tell her about my feelings sooner. I saw myself walking hand in hand with her on silly dates. I saw myself cuddling up to her and watching movies. I saw myself doing all the things I wanted to but never confessed. I saw myself and her in what could have been. As I saw these things I wanted nothing more than for Ann to squeeze my hand back. I wanted her to wake up with that stupid smile on her face and say some fool-hardy comment about the hospital room or everyone watching her like she's dying. I wanted nothing more than for everything to be okay. However, this selfish wish did not come true, as most selfish wishes don't. Instead, I was granted the deafening sound of the long drawn out heart rate monitor signaling the success of her father's goal. Then, as her hand did not squeeze mine, my reality settled itself around me and my mom's hand tightened instead, signaling the victory of the true reality.

Fifteen

After

The last time my mom wanted to buy me a suit, I was thirteen and nervously preparing for the eighth grade social. This is the equivalent to a senior year prom as a middle schooler. Now, my mom wanted to take me to get a suit for the Paige's funeral. This is not the equivalent of a senior year prom. My mom tried to treat it like an exciting outing but knew it was too soon. It would be a little while before I got excited about anything. Funeral preparations were all too familiar to my mom. I knew she was relieved that the only real preparations she had to make was my suit. However, I wasn't convinced that Ann would want people to be wearing suits and fancy dresses to her funeral. Knowing Ann, she would want people to comfortably mourn. Then again, funerals are not for the dead.

Eventually the day came around and I could no longer avoid the reality. It took place in our church because my family stepped up and offered the space to the family that remained living.

Observation: Ann did not have many remaining relatives who were alive.

Analysis on observation: Maybe there were more relatives who had not bothered to attend the funeral

Conclusion: I'm not sure.

It was a very long and annoying ceremony seeing as both of them had to be recognized and as the pastor put it, "celebrated." "We are not here to mourn the loss of two people who were very dear to us but celebrate the lives that they did have. They were honest, kind, and always brought a smile to all of our faces." He pulled out the most cliché thing to say at a funeral and because of that, I rolled my eyes. Of course, my mother pushed on my arm and shook her head. I love this woman with everything I have, but she doesn't quite understand everything that I am feeling now. I looked back towards the pastor and continued to listen to his clichés. "We know from our latest sermon series that light expels darkness and darkness is only true darkness when light is completely absent. These amazing people were lights in a lot of our lives and now we feel like we are in darkness. However, their light will continue to shine in us and will continue to expel that looming darkness." At this point I wanted to throw up and I thanked God and his ever-shining light that the sermon was over quickly. Now, it was time to pay our last respects.

Both coffins were in the front of the church and I entered the line of uncomfortable people not wanting to go through this process. Could I blame them? I didn't want to be there either. I didn't want to pay my last respects to them. I had already paid my respects back at the hospital. The last I would see of Ann would be her alive, not dead. However, I went through the paces and paid my respects like I am supposed to do. I went by each coffin and put my hand on them. I closed my eyes, shielding myself from the sight of the dead and acted like I was inspired by the words of the pastor, spoken just moments before. According to the pastor, this was not their final resting place. Their final resting place was in our hearts and our memories. While really cheesy and still cliché, I wanted to believe this was true. Ann and her mother were not pieces of flesh completing meaningless tasks, they were people that we all knew and we all loved. They were people who had a purpose and they were people who had aspirations. I still have an unwavering belief and a strong faith in God, because He is not the one who ripped them out of this world. While their time here may have been brief, I was given the amazing honor of getting to know them for the time that I did, and I have God to thank for that. After coming to the realization that I was turning into my pastor, I told my mom I was ready to leave, and we did. We headed out of the church and got into our car with every intention of skipping the burial part of the service. However, I couldn't, and I told her that I couldn't.

"I'm sorry, Mom, I need to go. It's a lot harder to say goodbye to her than I expected, and I can't let her do this on her own." My mom understood, and we headed towards the cemetery as I gathered myself to finally begin to accept what was happening.

"How are you doing, honey?" My mom posed the question extremely cautiously. I mean, she knew I was incredibly upset, but she also knew that there wasn't really anything that she could do about all of it.

"I'm hanging in there, Mom. I really appreciate everything you've been doing for me and I love you very much." She smiled at that. I don't tell my mom I love her every day, and while I regret that, I really appreciate it when she smiles so widely when I do say it. I would be heartbroken if she began to expect it or if it did not make as much of an impact on her.

I stood next my mom at the burial and she grabbed my hand after the blessing had been given. As the coffins made their way into the ground I choked up, but respectfully held it in. After it was over, and we were dismissed, I pulled my suit jacket back on and followed my mom to the car.

When people experience a loss, the other people around them always say, "I'm sorry." They'll say, "I'm sorry for your loss," or "I feel your pain," or the worst thing, "Do you want to talk about it?" No. I don't want to talk about it. No. You don't feel my pain. And why on God's green earth are *you* sorry about it? Did you cause the death? Is it because of you that I am grieving? No? In that case, shut your damn mouth and let me grieve alone. God knows I've done everything else alone.

God. Ever since it happened I've felt closer to Him. I would allow *Him* to apologize to me. If He said, "I'm sorry for your loss," I would actually understand why He said that. I would believe Him, too. If He said, "I feel your pain," I would actually believe Him. I would even talk to Him about it, if I was able to understand the reason behind the incident. However, it is not for my place to know, I just need to trust Him. I just need to trust that things will get better. I sure hope things will get better soon because I can't continue like this.

People say they experience grief more often than they actually do. They experience grief at the loss of a job, a harsh breakup, or a bad test. They need to grow up. The Webster Dictionary definition of grief is: deep sorrow, especially caused by someone's death. I'm sorry about your job, you'll find another one. I'm sorry about your breakup, you'll find someone else. I'm sorry about your test, maybe next time. What the hell are people supposed to say to me? I'll find someone else? It's not about finding; it's about being found.

Immediately after I got home, there was a lot of local media attention. Seeing as we were closer than most people were, the news had been knocking on our door very frequently. They had been asking me about the last time we saw each other or if I knew what was going on the whole time? I couldn't answer that question honestly, which surrounded me with an aura of suspicion. They had to understand how difficult it would be for me to recall any memories with them, right? *Obviously, we were close. Obviously, I am distraught. Obviously, this is not a newsworthy story. Please, leave me alone and allow me to lament.*

The milieu of Middleton was completely transformed into a somber atmosphere. Before, there were people walking busily along the streets and carrying groceries and sure about the future and the upcoming events that were to take place. But after, it hasn't been the same. People still needed to eat so they still walk around busily with groceries, but there was an uncertain feeling that filled the air now. No one was sure of what was to come. With the incident happening so suddenly, no one could be certain of anything anymore. A void was left in the middle of the streets that was usually home to gossip and normality. No one was sure when things will get back to normal or if they ever would.

I walked out of my house a few days after the funeral for the first time in a long time. I looked down at my bare feet, I hadn't even bothered to put on shoes. Those sorts of humane things didn't matter to me right now. I began walking down the sidewalk, away from my house and toward the site of the incident. I looked down again, but this time at the cracking sidewalk. I half smiled as I remembered the inanity of the superstition that followed the cracks on the sidewalk. As we grew up we would try our best to avoid the cracks. Now, about twelve years later, those six-year-old obstacles have gotten a lot larger. We still find ourselves walking down life's road and avoiding the cracks that are in the road. Sometimes, as Middleton learned, the cracks are unavoidable, and when they get stepped on, you and everyone around you is affected. While I continued to walk,

I looked around at the familiar faces that I have grown up seeing. I've grown so used to them that I've begun to take them for granted. No one was sure when things would get back to normal, and it took me by surprise when I started to see the tension slip away from the streets and down into the insignificant cracks in the sidewalk, acting like a drain in the bathtub. Laughter started to fill the streets once again and the ridiculous gossip from neighbors were fueled by silly whispers in the air. It seemed like only a few weeks later and everyone had forgotten. Everyone had moved on so soon. The life that mattered so much to me, didn't seem to matter to everyone else. Sure, they were sad, but they had moved on. *Good for them,* I thought bitterly. It wouldn't be that easy for me.

Ann's light would not continue to grow. In fact, it would slowly begin to fade. I would force myself to look at pictures of her that I had on my phone to remind myself what she looked like. However, without her personality, her light could not shine. As difficult as it would be, I would have to move on.

However, after everything that I had been through recently, after losing my mind, almost dying in the car accident, losing Ann and her mother, I had begun to see things more clearly. I grabbed my original copy of *Life's Little Instruction Book* and sat on the porch across from her now desolate house. You couldn't tell by looking at the outside that there were years of suffering within the walls. I flipped through the pages of Harry's book. They were the same pages that I had read an infinite amount of times since her passing. However, this time, the pages said something different to me. H.

Jackson Brown Jr. attempted to put an entire lifetime of "instructions" into a book and I had started to believe that he had successfully done it. A book is traditionally supposed to tell a complete story. Maybe it is just a part of a whole idea split into different sagas. Sometimes it jumps back and forth between two different times. No matter how the book is set up, it still completes a story sooner or later. *Life's Little Instruction Book* is no exception. It tells the complete story of a person who had a successful and content life. The main character is never mentioned nor, does it really have a protagonist at all. The rising conflict is the threat of a life that is not fulfilling, and Brown gives everyone the instructions on how to conquer that demon. The same is true for everyone. We are all given our own stories to write at birth. We get to choose how to write it and who gets to read it. Each day that we have an adventure, or an idea, or we say something (anything), it all gets recorded into our publicated legacy. Ann's book was well versed and exciting. She lived a full life in the eighteen years that she was given. While perusing the familiar book, I began to think about what my publicated legacy looked like thus far. Was it exciting? No. It was a lot of me doing my homework and working. Was it well versed? No. Is that a bad thing? Not necessarily. Up until traveling to Nashville I had never followed Brown's advice to explore, dream, and discover. Ann did. She was an explorer. She was a dreamer. She was a discoverer of all things. That is why I loved her and will continue to love her. I will continue my life with her book always close to me. When I am able, I will open it up for inspiration and insight to an exciting life. Her fictitious publicated legacy is available to all of those who knew her. Now, it is up to me to mend my publicated legacy. I needed to begin writing a life that God can be proud of and I can be proud of. I don't think I would call it an instruction book though. Everyone is allowed to use the gifts God gave them to craft their individual lives and that's what I've been lacking. I had spent the past eighteen years, looking up to Ann so much, that I'd forgotten to live my own life. I'd been too preoccupied trying to plagiarize her publicated legacy that I'd neglected my own and my readers have suffered. I got up from the bench and began to make my way back to my house.

Observation: Middleton is a lot smaller once you've travelled away from home.

Analysis on Observation: It will continue to get smaller and smaller as I travel further away.

Conclusion: Home will never be the same.

I found myself back in front of my house. I stared at the same door that I had walked through so many times and had taken it for granted. In the least cliché way, I was walking through a new chapter of my life. Those few weeks had been the awkward transition between the chapters. I'd focused so much on the before that it was finally time for me to focus on the after, and even more importantly, the present. Everything that would soon happen, would go down in my legacy.

I didn't feel like I could be hopeful. I didn't feel like I could be happy. I felt like I could just be. I couldn't figure out how long it would take me to get over her death, if I ever would. I couldn't stop living because of it and I'm sure she wouldn't have wanted me to do that. Every decision I would make after, is what I will leave behind. I couldn't help but get scared, but I knew I couldn't remain on that porch for the rest of my life. Just by looking at my house from the outside, you couldn't tell that my house was full of ghosts. It was full of Ann's ghosts as well as my father's ghosts. The interesting things about architecture, is that it covers up chaos, similar to the skin on our bodies. Before walking into my house, I instinctively checked the mailbox that was stationed on the left side of our door near our door bell. I was surprised to find an envelope and a package that was addressed to me. I recognized the return address immediately and quickly opened the envelope before walking inside.

Blake,

What an honor it was for you to stay at our house for the past few days. I am deeply humbled and quickly reminded how great the people in this world can become. You have given more to Rosemary and I than I could have ever hoped for. In fact, things have felt off since you have left, and we would love for you to return at your earliest convenience. Rosemary would also like me to add that she and I wake up every morning and immediately check on the progress of your tomato plant. It continues to grow every day and it makes us very happy. We hope that while the tomato plant prospers you are prospering as well.

A little bit of unfinished business exists between us, however, in regard to your quote. I hope you have found the comfort you were looking for, whether that be in the form of the origin or the acknowledgment that the quotes existence outweighs its origin story. However, between you and me, I was not the one who should be credited with this quote. It was my mother who originally had spoken the words to me as she prepared me for my life. As a father, I wrote Life's Little Instruction Book for my children in hopes that they see the same beauty of the world that I have also seen. This was inspired by my mother and father's kind words to me as I grew up and prepared to take on the world. I hope I can inspire you to pass on the knowledge and beauty of this world to those who will one day look up to you and call you Dad. 'Live so that when your children think of fairness, caring, and integrity they think of you.'

Enclosed in the package is a copy of Life's Little Instruction Book with a few added quotes that Rosemary and I believe are missing from the previous prints. We have also taken the time to acknowledge the author of the added quotes so as not to confuse anyone who may read it after you. Thank you again for giving us the opportunity to spend a few days with you and learn from you.
"You've given me confidence, friendship, love, and above all hope. Hope for myself, hope for the future, and hope for the beauty of this world." – Blake Harper

Your fan,

Harry

With shaking hands, I opened the enclosed package and immediately recognized the leather-bound copy of Brown's book. Next to it, in the box was a beautifully ripened tomato. I flipped to the dedication page and saw an addendum in Mr. Brown's handwriting.

To Blake – Thank you for teaching me the value of tomato seeds.

I smiled and flipped to the end of the 1560 quotes by Mr. Brown and saw more of his handwriting. It read:

#1561: *Put others first, but don't forget to take care of yourself. – Blake Harper*

#1562: *Find someone you want to share the world with. It is wide, and it will take two to see everything, I think. – Blake Harper*

#1563: *Amen? – Blake Harper*

Carl Bard was credited with the following quote: "Though no one can go back and make a brand-new start, anyone can start from now and make a brand-new ending." That is what I intended to do. With my new copy of *Life's Little Instruction Book* in hand and a new-found motivation to begin writing my publicated legacy, I grabbed the door handle and walked inside.

Present

Explore. Dream. Discover.

Explore. Dream. Discover.

Acknowledgments

I am incredibly excited about the beginning of this journey. I have worked on this piece for many years and am excited for people to be able to experience it.

I am indebted to my parents for helping me and motivating me throughout this entire journey. Thank you for being wonderful readers with great advice and critiques.

I am forever thankful for my muse. Without her most of this would have been impossible. Thank you, Maddie, for allowing me a destination to write towards.

Special thanks to Erin Oakes, Mary Eilerman, and Rebecca Conover for the wonderful editing.

I am thankful for H. Jackson Brown and his wonderful quotes that inspired this entire journey.

Finally, thank you, for reading this piece of fiction that I eventually concocted. I hope you enjoy it as much as I have enjoyed writing it.

Explore. Dream. Discover.

About the Author

Danny Bitter is incredibly excited to make his writing debut with *Explore. Dream. Discover.* He has studied political science, social studies education, music, and French at Southeast Missouri State University in Cape Girardeau, Missouri. He is an avid reader, pianist, singer, and carrot eater.

Though Danny Bitter doesn't have a lot of accomplishments in literature, he has many other accomplishments in life. These include, learning to juggle, going to college, scoring an amazing significant other, and finishing a book. He desperately hopes you enjoyed his story and that you may be interested in his other books that he will write.

Interested in how you can help Danny Bitter? You can do 2 things. First, follow him on social media! Second, write a positive review of this book. If you found it enjoyable, tell other people about it! Spread the word of this tomato filled journey. Thanks!

Twitter: @banielditter

Instagram: @banielditter

Explore. Dream. Discover.

Explore. Dream. Discover.

Made in the USA
Lexington, KY
02 August 2018